About the Author

The author's bottomless intellectual curiosity and boundless energy have spawned an eclectic career that has seen him constantly reinventing himself. Senior Partner in a major law firm. Chief Executive Officer of numerous health care organizations. Managing Member of an investment group focused on tax exempt bonds. Faculty member at a renowned school of public health. Author of scores of articles, a non-fiction book on health care, and two previous novels: *Mending Wall* and *Paradise Redeemed*. Member of many prestigious boards. Angel investor in promising start-ups that he felt could make a difference in people's lives. He has always been happiest when doing something productive, whether building a company or a dry stone wall. And yet, he never lost sight of his humble roots and connection to "those left behind," recognizing that human relationships are at the very core of all that matters in this world, whether marriage, family, business or country. He lives with his wife, Anne, on a horse farm in the coastal region of Massachusetts north of Boston known as the "North Shore."

"Beyond Las Vegas" is the ultimate road trip leading to revelation. Enjoy the ride.

AArON:
   ENJOY THE RIDE!.

BEYOND LAS VEGAS

Thomas Reardon

BEYOND LAS VEGAS

Vanguard Press

Vanguard Press is an imprint of
Pegasus Elliot Mackenzie Publishers Ltd.
www.pegasuspublishers.com

First Published in 2025

Vanguard Press
Sheraton House Castle Park
Cambridge England

Printed & Bound in Great Britain

Dedication

For my family: without whom, nothing.

Acknowledgments

I deeply appreciate the review and critique of the manuscript by my brothers, Rusty and Tim; introduction to the seductive allure of "Craps" by my friend Chrissy Lang; the insightful comments of dear friends Kathy Anderson and Pat Maykuth; and the contributions of my biggest critic and supporter—my wife, Anne

Chapter 1
The Great Red Shark

As he spooled the green garden hose into the brushed blue hose pot near the front stoop of their modest, three-bedroom ranch house, she eased through the screen door and paused to survey the newly wet marigolds along the stark concrete border of the foundation. The bold orange of the marigolds struggled to peek through the uncut dead, brown foliage from the single row of tulips that had flowered in spring. The air was hot and humid—typical Missouri weather in July. The window air conditioner in their bedroom was broken with a new one on back order—making sleeping a nightly ordeal. Their one saving grace was that 2023 was not a year for cicadas. The combination of open windows and the high pitch whine of cicadas auditioning for mates can be torture for, as Brits would say, the "knackered."

Approaching him with a sneer that reflected not only a visceral disdain but a weariness that had nothing to do with lack of sleep, Tammy sniped, "I'm glad to see you still have a pulse. This is the first time I've seen you excited about anything in years. I can't believe it; I finally get to meet the golden boy—the 'Superman' who can do no wrong."

Practically spitting, Steve shot back, "Jesus Christ, Tammy. Can you at least try and appear to be nice—if only for a little while?"

He could feel his acid reflux beginning to well up as he braced himself for the inevitable burn that would carve a well-worn and familiar path through his chest.

"Craig's text a few minutes ago said he'll arrive shortly. He's only going to be here briefly before we hit the road."

"You haven't seen Craig Wells since college, twenty-five years ago. What makes you think he hasn't changed? You certainly have."

"So have you, Tammy. So have you," Steve said, his words doled out with a dollop of bitterness. "As to Craig, you'll see. He's one of a kind. He's made millions with his private equity firm and can do anything he wants. He's living the dream."

"Your dream, Steve. Money begets money," Tammy replied dismissively. "He's always lived a privileged life—not being able to attend our wedding because he was sailing to the Marqueses. I sometimes wonder why you didn't go with him."

"Don't go there, Tammy."

"I'm still surprised that he ended up here at Mizzou. It must have been a culture shock for someone from the posh Upper East Side of Manhattan."

"As I've told you before, Craig came to Mizzou to play basketball. It's the only Division One school that recruited him. He was a star; I was a benchwarmer. Even though we came from different worlds, we became best friends."

"Then why haven't you seen each other in a quarter of a century?" Tammy challenged. "It sounds like a friendship of convenience confined to a short period of time and place, or—you're living in an illusion."

"Thanks, Tammy. I really appreciate your thoughtfulness," Steve replied as his shoulders slumped— no longer combative but subdued. Her words hurt; there was more than a hint of truth to her allegation. He and Craig had talked from time to time over the years, but in fact there hadn't been an effort to get together. The impending road trip to Las Vegas was a fantasy—a lark conjured up by Craig to search for the "American Dream" pursued by "Duke" and "Gonzo" fifty-two years ago in Hunter S. Thompson's book, *Fear and Loathing in Las Vegas*. [i]

"Tell me again—when will you be back? The kids will want to know."

"Will they? And how about you, Tammy? Do you want to know?"

"That goes without saying," Tammy replied, her eyes narrowing to slits.

"Maybe that's part of our problem—too much goes without saying," Steve replied angrily, suddenly belligerent again. "The plan is to be back next Tuesday— a week from today—but that's fluid. Not sure if we'll drive or Craig will ditch the car and we'll fly. I'll let you know."

"That would be nice," Tammy said sarcastically, her upper lip curled in an involuntary display of disapproval.

Just then a bright red 1973 Chevrolet Caprice convertible rolled slowly down their quiet, traffic-free street that was shaded by tree branches interlocked like hands clasped in prayer. After hesitating periodically as the driver checked mailboxes for the surname "Ehrlich," the car pulled into their driveway.

It was Craig Wells. From Steve's viewpoint, it didn't look like Craig had aged at all. He was still tall and handsome, dark brown hair without a fleck of gray, steely blue eyes that looked like they could see through walls— just like 'Superman.' Craig was clearly physically fit with his trademark cleft chin that had mesmerized so many co-eds, still chiseled as if in marble. He practically leaped from the car as he rushed to greet and hug Steve in a long embrace—not even attempting to cloak the hug in an outward display of "acceptable" male heterosexual affirmation by patting Steve's back.

Steve responded with a vigorous hug but, in sharp relief, patted Craig repeatedly on the back.

Steve felt a pang of shame. He had let himself go: a good thirty pounds overweight, balding—the remaining wisps of light brown hair turning a muted gray—and a softness to his features consistent with a complete lack of exercise and overeating to satisfy a need unrelated to hunger. There were times that he looked into the mirror when shaving and simply didn't recognize the six-foot-five, two hundred and fifty pound "Pillsbury Doughboy" staring back at him.

Craig was dressed in chinos, a navy blue Ralph Lauren polo shirt, and loafers—sans socks. Steve felt a self-conscious sting inasmuch as he was wearing an old pair of jeans and a ratty T-shirt advertising a local auto body shop. Tammy had cautioned him on his choice of apparel, but he had been defiant—letting it slide.

As Steve inspected the car while stewing quietly in his embarrassment and an intense apprehension of spending time with someone he hadn't seen in years—someone whom he revered as an almost mythic character—Craig introduced himself to Tammy. He noted that she was a good head and a half shorter than Steve, had straight brown hair cut pragmatically in a jaw-length bob, and the classic pear shape of many middle-aged women. Belying any impression of ordinariness, her intense, clamshell-colored eyes jumped out, reflecting a quick intelligence.

"Tammy, it's so great to meet you after all these years. Steve and I don't talk often, but you and the kids are always the foremost topics on his mind when we do."

"Thanks, Craig. It's nice to meet you as well. Can you come in to visit for a bit—maybe get something to eat?"

"I'd love that, Tammy, but I've already been on the road for six hours, and it will take us two to three hours to get to Kansas City. Let's plan to schedule some time on our trip back."

"That would be nice," Tammy said while biting her tongue, stifling any mention of Steve's earlier comment that the two of them might fly home—Craig to New York City; Steve to Columbia, Missouri—rather than drive.

"I can't believe it," Steve practically shouted while caressing the car as he circled it. "Is it the 'Great Red Shark?' How did you find it?"

"It's not the actual Red Shark, which is on exhibit in Las Vegas at—here's a surprise—the 'immersive' cannabis-themed museum called the 'Cannabition' inside the Planet 13 Complex. That's a must-see on our 'trip'— pun intended," Craig snickered. "I deal regularly with a car guy. He tracked this beauty down in Highland Park, Illinois. I flew into Chicago last night and picked it up this morning."

Impressed, Steve asked, "How did you get the owner to part with it?"

"Everyone has a price," Craig said cynically.

"I have a question," Tammy said as she furrowed her brow. "Not to rain on your parade, but I'm wondering how a 1973 Chevy could be the 'Red Shark' since *Fear and Loathing in Las Vegas* was published in 1971."

Steve was taken aback by the question. Not only did he not know the answer; he was embarrassed that Tammy had challenged his friend by asking.

Chuckling, Craig said, "Good question, Tammy. A 1973 Chevy Caprice convertible was gifted to Hunter S. Thompson by friends. It was the car he lusted after and became his 'Red Shark.' Besides, neither Thompson nor I would ever let facts get in the way of a good story."

"Speaking of Thompson—Steve, you've assured me that there will be no use of drugs on this trip," Tammy said forcefully. Turning to Craig and locking onto his eyes with an unflinching stare, she asked pointedly, "Do you concur?"

Nodding his head with a suddenly serious look, Craig replied reassuringly, "I concur wholeheartedly. You never know what you're going to get today. From what I've been reading, fentanyl, which can kill you, and large animal tranquilizers, which can cause skin lesions that can result in amputations, are frequently mixed with other drugs."

With a rueful grin, he added, "Damn—I guess there's no honor among drug dealers nowadays."

"Besides," Craig said, "I was struck by a passage in the book where Duke observes that drugs are almost irrelevant in a town where you can wander into a casino at any time of day or night and see the crucifixion of a gorilla on a flaming cross that turns into a pinwheel above the gaming tables."

"Thanks," Tammy said. "*The New York Times* anointed it the 'dope book' of the decade, and I just wanted to be sure."

"Grab your stuff, Steve, and let's hit the road. Tammy, it's really great to finally meet you. Sorry I didn't get a chance to meet your son and daughter—George and Jennifer, isn't it?"

"Yes. George is fourteen and Jennifer twelve," Tammy replied. She was surprised that Craig knew their names. *Had Steve actually talked about them in conversations with Craig, or had Craig simply been gracious and classy enough to ask Steve as they planned their trip?* "They're both at swimming lessons right now. I'm sure they'll be disappointed to have missed you since Steve has often talked glowingly about your time together in college. Maybe on the trip back."

"I'd like that, Tammy."

With that, Steve threw his duffel bag and backpack into the trunk of the car after rearranging several large trash bags overflowing with all sorts of plastic.

"What's the plastic for?" Steve asked.

"God knows," Craig said. "I didn't see the plastic until I transferred my duffel bag from the backseat to the trunk this morning while stopping to take a leak and get a cup of coffee. We'll ditch the trash bags as soon as we see one of those plastic recycling locations."

Steve gave Tammy a cursory peck on her turned cheek and hopped into the car to ride 'shotgun.' "See you in a week," he said.

Tammy suppressed the words "Oh Goody," instead calling out, "Have fun," as the car pulled out of the driveway.

"I haven't been in Columbia in years," Craig said. "Let's do a quick drive downtown and around the campus. By the way, really cool sleeves, Steve. When did you get into ink?"

"I joined a local band after college. I played guitar and sang backup vocals. Some of the guys in the band decided to get tattoos, so I joined them. We were trying to create a 'look.' Tammy hates it."

"So what kind of tattoo style is that?"

"The style is called a 'fine line' because of its simple, clean lines that are aesthetically pleasing," Steve replied.

"What the hell is that tattoo on your right forearm?" Craig asked. "It looks like a pinecone."

"Our band was called the 'Third Eye,' and we all got the same tattoo on our right arms. It's a depiction of the pineal gland in the center of the brain, which looks like, and was named for, the pinecone."

"Okay. You lost me. Why the pineal gland?" Craig said with a look of bewilderment.

"The 'third eye' is considered the center of energy and spiritual connection in religions like Hinduism, Buddhism, and Taoism and can supposedly be opened by activating the pineal gland through yoga and meditation."

"Oh my God." Craig laughed. "It just occurred to me. If I recall correctly, Duke and Gonzo feared the psychoactive properties of pineal gland extract from a living human being that was presumably taken by violent means. Is that what you guys were thinking when you named the band?"

"Purely coincidental," Steve replied. "I had forgotten that allusion in the book. Can't say I ever had the extract. Have you?"

"No way," Craig said. "Talk about not trusting a dealer—how about not trusting the method of extraction?"

"Do you still play?" Craig asked.

"Nah. The band wasn't going anywhere, and we broke up after a couple of years. I lost interest in my guitar, and the guys and I just drifted apart. At some point we lost contact."

Pausing for a minute, Steve continued, "Jimmy Buffett had a song about a tattoo being an everlasting memory of a momentary impulse. [ii] I've often thought about getting mine removed, and now that you've reminded me of pineal gland extract, there's a little more urgency to following through before anyone else makes the connection. Who knew tattoos would go mainstream? It's one of the only things about me that my kids think is cool."

"Watch out, Pal. If they haven't already, I suspect the kids will begin bugging you about getting their own."

Sighing audibly, Steve said, "It's already started. Fortunately, Missouri law won't allow a person to get a tattoo until they're eighteen—but that's coming soon. So far I've said 'no,' but it does seem hypocritical. Tammy is adamantly opposed. I'm not looking forward to the coming clash of wills."

"Who knows—maybe George will change his mind in four years—particularly if you don't make a big deal of it before then. Getting yours removed and acknowledging it as a 'mistake' might help."

"Wise counsel. I hope you're right," Steve said.

Leaning back on the split bench seat of the Caprice, Steve marveled: "Man, I'd almost forgotten about these kinds of seats. It feels like I'm reclining on a 'La-Z-Boy.' And the loose suspension makes it seem like we're floating on air—which is great if this dinosaur doesn't have to make any hairpin turns. The vinyl seats are so retro that it makes me think of college when we could cruise down to that old root beer stand near campus with the servers on roller skates."

"I love it. I haven't thought of that image in years— our own slice of *American Graffiti*. [iii] Having said that, I've been in the car half a day already, and you'll find out that the novelty wears off quickly, particularly since the vinyl not only feels 'plasticky,' but is hot and sticky in the sun. The good news is that vinyl cleans up better than leather or fabric, and since it's white, will make it easier to see and remove any random vomit from drinking on this trip," Craig chortled.

Laughing as well, Steve said, "Still finding silver linings, huh, Craig?"

"You bet, Bro. It certainly beats the alternative," Craig replied.

As they pulled onto Broadway, the "main drag" in town, Craig was surprised to see that things hadn't changed much. Of course Broadway is in the historic district, and so preservation was understandable. Washing over him in the welcome summer breeze, he felt a warm nostalgia for the classic Midwestern town, with the facades of the mostly brick buildings generally no more than two or three stories high, and where people you meet on the street look you in the eye and say hello. He was excited to see that some of the popular student bars that he and Steve had frequented while at Mizzou were still there. Twenty-one was the minimum age for alcohol in Missouri, but they all had fake I.D.s. And there was a thriving Greek-life on campus with dozens of fraternities that regarded the law as merely a suggestion, earning Mizzou a well-deserved reputation as a "party school."

Driving slowly down memory lane, something that was seemingly out-of place caught Craig's eye—a restaurant called "Seoul Taco." The colors of the South Korean flag filled in the "o" in the word "Seoul."

Craig pulled the Red Shark into a parking space outside the restaurant as he said excitedly, "I can't believe it. That's the blue and red 'taegeuk' at the center of the South Korean flag. It represents the duality of Heaven and Earth—in Columbia, Missouri of all places! I've heard of 'Asian fusion,' but 'Korean tacos?'"

"Change is coming even to Columbia, Missouri," Steve said grudgingly. "Coincidentally, the President of Mizzou also happens to be Korean-American."

"Fantastic! He must be incredibly well qualified to break through here in 'Mayberry,'" Craig teased.

"Maybe," Steve conceded while scowling. "However, as conservative as Missouri is, creeping 'wokeism' is permeating all levels of society—even here. I really believe that white men are now being discriminated against and are the last group in America that can be joked about."

"What are you talking about?" Craig asked.

"I'll give you a vivid example," Steve replied. "A young African American woman was recently given tenure and appointed head of our history department, even though I've been teaching at Mizzou for years as an adjunct professor and have been passed over for promotions. We adjuncts work like dogs, are paid a paltry amount, and are treated poorly. I can't say anything, or I could be dismissed without a second thought—discarded like superfluous punctuation in the narrative of the school."

"Oh my God," Craig guffawed. "You've turned into a 'red neck.'"

"I've always been a 'red neck,'" Steve responded— also laughing. "I just have more 'real world' experience now. And you, Dude, have apparently become what we used to call a 'limousine liberal' and now a 'coastal elite.'"

"I would recognize that high pitched cackle of yours anywhere," Craig teased. "I thought you would grow out of it once you hit delayed puberty."

"Very funny," Steve replied while punching Craig on the shoulder. "How do you know about the South Korean flag?"

"I've spent some time in Seoul where my firm invested in a Korean company that's trying to become the Korean 'Amazon.'"

"Let's get some tacos for the road trip," Craig suggested. "I'm trying to imagine what Korean tacos could be."

The restaurant had several utilitarian metal tables and chairs inside but was basically a fast-food takeout joint with modest prices tailored to the budgets of university students. Menu offerings were listed on a large sign behind the counter. There were a variety of both Korean and Mexican choices, but something stood out: a so-called "Munchwrap Seoulpreme." It consisted of a flour tortilla layered with refried beans, spicy kimchi, cheddar cheese, a crispy corn tortilla shell, and a choice of protein (with tofu as an option), sesame seeds, green onion, and "gochujang" sour cream.

"What in the hell is 'gochujang' sour cream?" Steve asked.

"It's delicious, Craig replied. "My recollection is that gochujang includes red chili pepper flakes, fermented soybeans, and sticky rice that's also fermented. Think of it as a spicy, thick ketchup."

Craig asked the gawky, acne-festooned teenager behind the counter if the proprietor was on site—thinking he could provide a much better description. Unfortunately, the Korean-American owner wasn't in; the counter person was a local kid who didn't have a clue about the ingredients.

Craig ordered two of the Munchwrap Seoulpremes to go.

Resuming their drive to the nearby University of Missouri campus, Craig asked, exaggerating his pronunciation of the suffix, "So is 'Otis Winthrop **the Third'** still teaching at Mizzou?"

"Yeah," Steve said. "Once someone gets tenure, they burrow in like a tick and won't let go. I bump into him from time to time at faculty meetings."

"What a pompous ass!" Craig exclaimed. "All I can think of when Otis comes to mind is Eddie Murphy's Saturday Night Live skit, where he goes underground masquerading as a white man and has to walk with a tight ass. I don't know what got me started, but no matter where I'm visiting in the world, I try to send Otis a cocktail napkin identifying a famous bar on which I've written, 'Fuck you, Otis!'"

Laughing, Steve replied, in disbelief, "How old are you?"

"Old enough to know better. But what the hell. On the bright side, if he kept them, Otis must have quite a collection of cocktail napkins at this point. 'Sidney's Peace

& Love Restaurant' in the British West Indies; Harry's New York Bar in Paris, where he can mingle with the ghosts of Ernest Hemingway and Humphrey Bogart; and on and on."

"Poor Otis," Steve said. "It sounds like a stunt we might have pulled at our fraternity."

Chuckling, Craig said, "Here's a news flash for you, Steve. The 'Frat Boy' culture still reigns supreme in the New York finance world. Besides, I simply can't resist the impulse. What an effete, condescending snob—ironic in that he's probably the only white man in America named Otis."

"How about his father and grandfather?" Steve replied while laughing. "Of course, you're illustrating my point about white men being fair game for jokes. Having said that, I have to admit that his Boston accent and odd formality really put me off at first."

"It wasn't a 'Southie' accent like you hear in the movies," Craig noted. "Rather, it had more of a Beacon Hill Brahmin intonation reflecting his uppity patrician roots."

"He isn't a bad guy," Steve said. "He was only ten or so years older than us, and it dawned on me, in retrospect, that he was trying to project gravitas. He was like an immigrant with a more formal social background than Midwesterners, but, unlike someone from a foreign country, we didn't cut him any slack."

"I hadn't thought of it that way. Maybe I should stop sending him bar napkins," Craig said, laughing. "But probably not. It's a tradition at this point."

They pulled the Red Shark up to the location of their fraternity: Lambda Chi Alpha.

Disoriented at first, Craig gasped, "Oh my God. This is the Taj Mahal. What happened to the old place?"

"Progress—I guess," Steve said. "The century old original was torn down a couple of years ago, and this 'new and improved' model was put up in its place. I thought you knew."

"No—I had no idea. I have to admit that the new house is beautiful," Craig said, "but it's shocking to see the original gone. I guess I shouldn't have expected my memories to be preserved in amber."

"Yeah," Steve acknowledged, but added sarcastically, "But, I'm sure you're pleased to see that the old power station is still across the street continuing to enhance the curb appeal of Lambda Chi Alpha."

"Very gratifying," Craig chortled.

The two of them took 'selfies' sitting in the Red Shark with the pristine, white wood-clad fraternity house as background.

"I'm trying to picture the original and reminisce about our time here. Man, does that bring back memories or what?" Craig asked.

"I'll say. Lambda Chi Alpha got suspended for a couple of weeks not long ago," Steve mentioned. "Sigma Chi actually got suspended permanently."

"I wonder how we avoided permanent suspension during our time here?" Craig said while chuckling.

"It's a miracle," Steve said. "Do you remember the time you, Tommy Murtaugh, and I were blasted downtown one night and the local police took us into 'protective custody?' I can still hear Tommy yelling from the jail cell: 'Ociffer, Ociffer. We're not drunk,' as we intermittently spit water over the top of the wall into the next cell while giggling the entire time."

"That was a simpler time when the police didn't fear for their lives and could actually 'serve and protect' out-of-control college students," Craig mused. "We slept it off and were never charged. I'm not sure what would happen today."

"I just remembered something," Craig said as he hopped out of the car and went to retrieve some items from his duffel bag in the trunk.

Returning to the driver's seat, Craig donned a Yankees ballcap and said to Steve, "Put some of this sunscreen on or you'll look like a boiled lobster by the time we get to Kansas City. And pick one of these 'loser' ballcaps. They're official MLB gear for the Kansas City Royals and St. Louis Cardinals."

Steve shot back, "'Losers?' The Royals won the World Series in 2015, and the Cardinals won in 2011. The Yankees haven't won since 2009. Who's the 'loser?' And speaking of 'losers,' when was the last time the Giants or Jets won a Super Bowl? The Chiefs have won two of the last four."

"A mere flash in the pan," Craig teased. "The Yankees have won twenty seven World Series. The Royals have been more like a farm team over the years."

"Since we're going to Kansas City, I'll wear the Royals ballcap," Steve declared defiantly. "You're not going to wear that Yankees hat there are you? You're just looking for trouble."

"I'll risk it," Craig chuckled.

As they drove on, Craig noted a lot of new building on campus beyond the fraternity house, particularly involving the health system.

"Yeah," Steve observed. "The new Children's Hospital, that will cost about a quarter of a billion dollars, is under construction. There's a new indoor practice facility for the football team—among other things. I don't notice the change that much since it's gradual for me, but I can see how it could be a jolt for someone who hasn't been here for twenty-five years."

"I'll say," Craig said while sighing. "Nothing is forever. Speaking of which, I guess Mizzou is in the big time now that it's in the SEC. And both Texas and Oklahoma are about to join after leaving the Big 12 Conference. What's going to be left?"

"Unclear," Steve said nostalgically. "Money talks and old rivalries, just like traditional values, are being torn apart."

Seeing a number of school banners as they drove around campus, Craig asked, "I have a question for you that I never thought about when we were in school. Why is 'Mizzou' spelled with the letter 'Z' when there's no 'Z' in 'Missouri?'"

"There are many theories," Steve answered. "The most popular is that it's a shortened version of the university's initials—which were originally MSU for Missouri State University."

"But there's no 'Z' in MSU," Craig protested.

"Why is it spelled 'fridge' when there's no letter 'D' in refrigerator?" Steve quipped.

Laughing, Craig said, "I guess some mysteries will never be solved. I still can't wrap my mind around the fact that Indiana sports teams are called 'Hoosiers.' What in the hell is a Hoosier?"

Driving around town beyond Broadway, Craig commented that Columbia seemed quite prosperous.

"It's the fastest growing city in Missouri," Steve said. "Education, health care, and insurance have created an economic boom that is largely recession proof."

Finally breaking away, the two of them headed for I-70 West, which they would follow for most of the trip. Just before they got to the on-ramp, Craig pulled into an ATM housed in a small brick facility attached to a Bank of Missouri branch.

"I've got cash if you need any, Craig," Steve offered.

"Thanks, but I have something else in mind," Craig replied as he opened the trunk, grabbed the trash bags, and "deposited" them in the structure that contained the ATM.

"What the hell are you doing?" Steve protested. "This isn't a plastic recycling site."

"It looks like one to me," Craig said, laughing mischievously. "Screw them if they can't take a joke."

Hopping back in the car, Craig announced breezily, "There's a cooler in the back seat. I filled it with ice and local craft beers I picked up in Highland Park this morning. Grab a couple of beers, and we'll eat our Korean tacos as we drive."

Fifteen minutes west of Columbia, they approached the bridge spanning the Missouri River.

"Holy crap!" Craig said as he pulled over just before the bridge to take in the view. "I hadn't realized that there was such a large gorge here. It's not the Grand Canyon but is pretty impressive."

As they sat in the open ragtop, the misting air wafting up from the river dropped the ambient temperature twenty to thirty degrees.

"How could you have not noticed, Dude? We went by bus to play Kansas and Kansas State every year and crossed the gorge."

"I don't know. I must have been playing cards or goofing off on the bus. I always flew into St. Louis coming to campus, and so wouldn't have crossed the river from that direction."

"It's amazing what we missed when we were only nineteen or twenty," Steve observed.

"Amen! I guess we aren't often granted a second chance, but here we are."

Sipping on his beer, Steve mentioned, "There's amazing, unspoiled scenery near here. I like to go to a place called Eagle Bluffs after church on Sunday and just sit and relax by the river, imagining what it was like in the days of Lewis and Clark."

"Does your family go with you?" Craig asked.

"They joined me at first, but the kids quickly lost interest—*too boring!* I go by myself most weekends for just an hour or so. Tammy feels obligated to stay home with the kids. I'm okay with that. The brief respite is relaxing and lets my mind wander."

"Good for you, Bro," Craig said. "Everything I've read says that time spent in nature is restorative."

"I guess so," Steve replied. "I don't know if you know it but the Missouri is the longest river in the country."

Incredulous, Craig said, "No. Not longer than the Mississippi."

"Google it. The headwaters of the Missouri are in Montana."

"Then why isn't it called the Montana River?"

"I'm not sure. The Missouri empties into the Mississippi in St. Louis. I guess the name comes from the state where the river ends."

"Come to think of it, a river near me that I cross to go skiing—the Connecticut River—begins in Northern New England but dumps into the Long Island Sound near Old Lyme and Old Saybrook, Connecticut. I'm impressed; I guess you learned something teaching history all these years," Craig said tauntingly as he took a healthy slug of his beer.

"Don't remind me," Steve replied with an exasperated sigh. "After all these years teaching and still sucking hind teat—completely expendable."

"Why don't you quit if you don't like it?" Craig asked.

"It's too late for me. I'm locked in at this point. I need the tuition relief I'll get from the position so the kids can go to Mizzou."

"Too late?" Craig scoffed. "What, are you—ninety years old?"

"I'm not sure where I'd go or what I'd do if I didn't teach at Mizzou," Steve replied.

"How about relocating? Are you willing to do that? Maybe I can help you find something."

"Tammy and the kids wouldn't like that—too many local roots. And, to be honest, I don't know if I could do it even if I found a new job. I guess I'm just a small town boy and always will be," Steve said.

As they pulled out to cross the bridge, Steve drained his beer and, while grabbing another one, tossed the empty can into the gorge.

"Oh my God," Craig said while bursting into laughter. "Not only are you a redneck but also a 'litter bug.'"

"Trust me on this one, Craig. We don't want to be pulled over with open beer cans."

"Okay. So how do you like your taco?" Craig asked. "Mine is great."

"Not so much," Steve replied. "The sauce is too spicy, and I don't like the kimchi. And what were you thinking, ordering tofu as the protein? Uggh! Another example of me being a small town boy, I guess."

"Looking at a map—yes, I have GPS, but I also have an old, hopelessly out-of-date Rand McNally Atlas that I study to get my bearings before a trip—Columbia appears to be smack dab in the middle of the State, equidistant between St. Louis and Kansas City," Craig observed.

"You have a good eye. In fact, maybe your third eye has been activated in anticipation of this trip," Steve said sarcastically. "Believe it or not, the exact midpoint between the two cities is 300 W Texas Ave in Columbia."

"Unreal," Craig stated. "By the way, I do plan to activate certain body parts during our adventure—but I never envisioned that the pineal might be one of them. Having said that, remember Duke's exhortation about no sympathy for the devil." [iv]

"I do remember," Steve said dreamily. "Something about buying the ticket and taking the ride. Sounds like a plan."

"This should be an interesting trip," Craig mused. "Las Vegas is way different than what Duke and Gonzo experienced fifty years ago. Of course, so is America. Remember the famous Las Vegas slogan: 'What happens in Las Vegas stays in Las Vegas.' Not anymore. Las Vegas was named the 'New All-American City' by Time Magazine in the mid-90s. It was 'Sin City' back in the day. Now it represents what America is becoming: excess, non-stop entertainment, immersive experiences, altered reality."

"I'll keep an open mind, but I'm not sure I buy that," Steve retorted, laughing. "I doubt we'll see a gorilla crucifixion at Arrowhead Stadium any time soon. But, as you said: this should be an interesting trip."

***

One four-pack and an hour into the trip, Craig marveled at the large number of starlings working the farms next to the highway.

"Yeah," Steve said. "We're not very good about family outings, but we do go out from time to time to see the starlings in the fall as they practice for their annual migration. A twisting, undulating flock flying as if one organism is called a 'murmuration' because it sounds like a murmur that ebbs and flows as the birds fly. Have you ever seen or heard one Craig?"

"Only on TV. It strikes me as magical. I'd love to see and hear a murmuration in person."

"It is magical," Steve replied. "Although native songbirds seem to be in trouble, starlings are tough transplants that have thrived in North America. My recollection is that an eccentric, wealthy socialite released a handful in Central Park a century ago because she wanted to see all the birds mentioned by Shakespeare represented in the new world. We're in the middle of the Mississippi Flyway for migrating birds. One of the attractive things about going out to see the murmurations is that the price of entertainment is right. Having said that, as the kids grow older, it's like pulling teeth to get them to join us."

"Understandable—although they'll remember it later in life," Craig said. "I have a question. Except for the occasional personal injury lawyer or farm insurance advertisements, the billboards seem to be dominated by 'pro-life' and 'pro-choice' positions. That's something we don't see back East."

"It's pretty intense," Steve said. "The pro-life advocates have the upper hand in Missouri, with the legislature recently restricting abortion. I'm not sure what the outcome would be if there was a referendum like those in Kentucky and Kansas where voters rejected constitutional amendments that would have allowed the legislature to curtail abortion rights. Evangelical Christians are a real political force out here."

"What is it with evangelicals?" Craig asked. "Since the Bible is quiet on the subject, my understanding is that back when Roe v. Wade was being decided, leading evangelical theologians punted on the issue, thinking it was largely a Catholic cause. Some even spoke favorably about the Supreme Court decision, saying it embraced their ideal of individual freedom. Now it's a cause célèbre."

"To be honest," Steve said, "I don't recall abortion being a big issue until relatively recently. I'm not sure what triggered the current focus."

"I read that it was only during the 1978 mid-term elections that evangelical leaders recognized that abortion was a powerful grassroots mobilization issue and began to champion the cause," Craig replied. "And that focus has only strengthened over time."

"Interesting," Steve replied. "And I thought I was the historian."

"It seems to me that as America has turned more and more secular with increasing numbers of people not attending church, politics has become the new religion for the non-observant, and evangelicals have reacted by trying to seize political power to impose their worldview," Craig said.

Craig continued, "Not only do we see certain states banning abortion—which appears to be a minority opinion among voters even in Red States—I just read that the

Texas Senate passed a bill that would require the Ten Commandments to be displayed in primary and secondary schools and that time should be put aside for Bible study. What about Muslims, Hindus, and non-believers?"

"Tammy and I are evangelicals," Steve said as he paused to let his revelation sink in. "She's into our church in a big way and is all-in on pro-life issues—although she's also in favor of exceptions for rape, incest, and the life of the mother. I can see both points of view on abortion. The thing that gives me pause—that kind of parrots your concern—is the talk I hear from Tammy and her friends about making America a 'Christian nation.'"

"What does that mean to you and Tammy?" Craig asked.

"In Tammy's case, I think she's simply talking about restoring traditional values. However, I understand that there are surging movements like 'The 7 Mountain Mandate' and the 'New Apostolic Reformation' that are the hard edge of Christian nationalism. [v] Have you heard of them?"

"Not much," Craig responded.

"I won't get into all the biblical underpinnings, but the bottom line is that the movements seek to control all seven spheres of society: family, religion, education, media, entertainment, business, and government—with no separation between church and state. Some of the people breaching the Capitol on January 6 apparently carried flags associated with the NAR."

"So what will we call this Christian nation? A 'Caliphate?' Will it be governed by Sharia Law?" Craig taunted.

"Ha! Ha! Very funny," Steve replied dismissively. "Just so you know, I'm not sure I trust 'true believers' of any faith."

"I thought all this was just loose talk," Craig said. "Thinking about it now, it's scary. I've read that over forty percent of Americans and over eighty percent of evangelicals think that America should be a 'Christian nation.' My fear is that, notwithstanding the embrace of personal freedom like being able to 'carry' a gun, what it really means is: 'Don't tell me what to do, but do as I say.'"

"I carry a gun," Steve mentioned nonchalantly.

Shocked, Craig practically shouted, "What? Do you have one on you now?"

"Yeah. In Missouri, you don't have to be licensed to carry—in fact, technically, there's no prohibition on toddlers carrying. I got licensed so that other jurisdictions would recognize my rights. Each of the States we'll be traveling to have 'open carry' laws and, if you're licensed, reciprocity as to concealed weapons."

"Good God," Craig said. "I'm sorry, but I think the Supreme Court got this one wrong. The right to carry arms in the Second Amendment modifies the language about a 'well-regulated militia, being necessary to a free state.' Most lawyers I know say that words are there for a reason, and yet this Court pretends that the reference has no meaning."

"The law is what the Supreme Court says it is," Steve replied firmly.

"Until it isn't," Craig shot back. "Even if one concedes the right to carry arms, shouldn't there be a balancing test: individual freedom versus community good? Why wouldn't everyone agree to background checks for example?"

"I agree with that," Steve replied. "I think the majority of gun owners agree with common sense controls."

"You mentioned that Missouri prohibits tattoos until a person is eighteen but has no age requirement for owning a gun. Does that make any sense?"

"Of course not. There should be minimum age requirements on both," Steve responded.

"But extreme views prevail," Craig said. "Why, for example, does anyone need a combat weapon like an assault rifle? They're not used for hunting but to kill people. Why not insist on the right to own a grenade launcher or a stinger missile? Why can't we draw a sensible line?"

"I also agree with that. Having conceded the point, believe it or not, there is a legitimate use for assault weapons in hunting."

"Oh man," Craig sighed. "I can hardly wait to hear this one."

"There are now more than nine million feral hogs loose in this country," Steve said. "Not only do they do incredible damage to crops and woodlands, they're opportunistic carnivores who prey on ground nesting birds and fawns hiding in the grass. If you shoot and kill one hog, the rest of the family group, called 'sounders,' quickly scatter. An assault weapon allows you to take them all out. Nevertheless, I'm in favor of reasonable limitations."

Chuckling, Craig said, "I didn't know about feral hogs. It's not a serious problem in Manhattan."

"From what I hear, it's very much a problem in Manhattan," Steve snickered. "It's just that the hogs are human."

"Very funny," Craig said while laughing. "More importantly, how about another beer?"

"Sounds good to me," Steve said as he reached into the cooler in the back seat and broke open a second four-pack.

"So what ever happened to Tommy Murtaugh? Do you ever hear from him?" Craig asked.

"I saw him at our fifth reunion. He was married and living in the Seattle area, working for Microsoft. It's the only reunion I attended. I'm not sure what he's doing now."

"How about Jimmy Lyons, Ed Bannon, and the other guys we used to hang out with?"

"No idea. I don't have a Facebook account and haven't kept in touch."

"I haven't kept in touch either," Craig said. "I never opened a Facebook account. You're the only person from college I've touched base with over the years."

"I guess we're both dinosaurs when it comes to social media." Steve smirked.

"Based on what I'm reading, I guess that's a good thing," Craig said. "I'm curious. Do you know what happened to Sophia Caputo? She was incredibly hot, and I liked her a lot but purposely avoided any long-term entanglements while in school."

"She wasn't just hot, Bro—she was smoldering. I would have loved to have hooked up with her but she was out of my league. Sophia didn't attend the fifth reunion, and I haven't heard of her for years."

Pausing for a minute, Steve asked, "I have a question for you. Unlike me, why did you make a decision, at twenty-two, to avoid any 'entanglements,' as you put it?"

"Life is short," Craig responded. "I wanted to experience the world before getting on with commitments that would tie me down, like marriage or family. I must say, from time to time I wonder about my decision, but there's no going back at this point."

Steve didn't reply as he thought about his own 'commitments.' He had simply done what his father and his father's father had done before him. At the time, it had never occurred to him that there was another way. Craig and he had made very different life decisions. Who had chosen the right path?

Chapter 2
"Kansas City, Kansas City"

As the two of them reached the outskirts of the city, Craig asked, "How come there are so many songs about Kansas City? Or is it just one song rearranged over and over again and covered by countless performers? And what's the story about '12th Street and Vine?'"

"Believe it or not," Steve responded enthusiastically. "For years, Kansas City was one of the hottest places in America for jazz and R&B. Count Basie formed his first orchestra at the legendary Reno Club, which was in the same neighborhood as 12th and Vine. Charlie Parker earned his 'Yardbird' nickname at the club. One of the busiest nightspots was the 'Orchid Club,' which was literally at 12th and Vine. Billie Holiday, Etta James and other greats performed there. It was also a major R&B venue with Ray Charles, Fats Domino and others appearing."

"Really? I had no clue," Craig replied. "But what about the song or songs about Kansas City?"

"Lieber and Stoller wrote their famous tune, 'Kansas City,' in 1952," [vi] Steve said. "More than three hundred versions of the song have been recorded by artists including Sammy Davis, Little Richard, Tom Jones, and the Beatles. It was an incredible time and place where

41

whites and blacks mixed easily, and music was the universal language that transcended racial and other barriers."

"So what happened?" Craig asked.

"Unfortunately, the neighborhood became neglected and was ultimately razed for urban renewal. The good news is that every time the song 'Kansas City' is played, '12th Street and Vine' lives again."

"That's a really cool way to think of it," Craig said. "How do you know all this?"

"Being a historian has some benefits." Steve chuckled. "There are still more than forty live music venues in Kansas City with something for everyone."

"Fantastic!" Craig enthused. "Let's get the concierge to set us up with tickets for some live music tonight after dinner. Speaking of dinner, I know that Kansas City is known for its distinctive barbeque and quality steaks. Any preference?"

"There's no question," Steve said emphatically. "There are more than one hundred barbeque joints in town. You can't really experience Kansas City without trying the barbeque. It starts with a dry rub, slow-smoked over a variety of woods, and is served with a thick, sweet sauce that includes tomatoes, molasses and brown sugar that makes it unique."

"I'm hungry already," Craig declared.

"By the way, where are we staying?" Steve asked. "And thanks for making and paying for all the lodging arrangements."

"My treat," Craig said. "I wanted to stay at the historic Rieger Hotel. I picked it initially because I read that Al Capone used to stay there when he was in town. The hotel is close to Union Station, and he could hightail it back to Chicago quickly if he needed to. Unfortunately, the hotel, its highly regarded restaurant, the 'Rieger Hotel Grill & Exchange,' and the 'Manifesto,' which apparently revived the 'speakeasy' scene in Kansas City, all closed permanently during the pandemic. The building is on the National Register of Historic Places and has been converted to condos."

"I've read about the Rieger. Sorry, we'll miss out on the experience. So where are we staying?" Steve asked.

"I thought about the casino hotels overlooking the Missouri River like Harrah's Kansas City, but then figured we'll get enough of that in Las Vegas. I decided to book us at the Hotel Indigo, a boutique hotel right downtown," Craig replied. "Incidentally, I reserved one room in each location with two queen size beds so that we can make sure that neither of us gets into trouble from excessive drinking—something I plan to do plenty of."

"Good thinking," Steve said. "I have a question. I know speakeasies were creatures of Prohibition, but I never knew why they were called that. Any idea?"

"I thought you were the historian, Steve," Craig teased. "As I understand it, because the proprietors wanted to make it difficult for the cops to find them, speakeasies were hidden behind secret panels in places like a hotel or were accessible through obscure side doors in an alley. The existence of a speakeasy was shared by word of mouth, and the bartender whispered to the patrons, 'Speak easy' to keep down any noise."

"I should have known," Steve said. "Let's try to find one after eating ribs and catching some music."

"I'm all in," Craig replied.

***

Sitting at Joe's 'Kansas City Bar-B-Que,' Craig and Steve gorged on baby back ribs washed down by draft 'Cypersonic C-Hops Double IPAs,' a local craft beer brewed by the local Boulevard Brewing Co. The beer had been recommended by their waitress, whose name, 'Marge,' was emblazoned on her white blouse.

"So what are you boys doing in town?" Marge asked as she bent down to serve a second round of beers with the top two buttons of her blouse undone, revealing an impressive cleavage.

"We're on our way to Las Vegas," Craig responded playfully. "We're just looking to have some fun."

"Kansas City is a great place to have fun," Marge bantered back, her eyes and body language flirtatious.

Marge was an attractive woman—probably in her early forties—with the telltale signs of a heavy smoker, including a husky voice, crow's feet around her eyes, and lines around her mouth. As the light hit her shoulder-length hair, Craig noticed that the hair near her temples was a lighter shade of brown than the rest, suggesting that she was using a touch-up hairstick that was not a perfect match. He also noticed that she wasn't wearing a wedding ring.

"Marge, I'm told that Missouri allows smoking in bars. Is it true? I haven't seen that in years," Craig asked.

"It is true—but only in designated smoking areas."

"How does that work?" Craig asked with a gleam in his eye. "It sounds like chlorinating only one end of a swimming pool."

All three of them laughed.

"Fair enough," Marge replied. "And it's not like we have 'morality police' enforcing the rules."

"We're headed to Knuckleheads Saloon after dinner. Do you know if they allow smoking?"

"They do. You'll love Knuckleheads. It's really cool with a number of live music stages. Too bad it's Tuesday. They usually only have live music Wednesday through Sunday."

"We lucked out. Apparently, they occasionally schedule an act on Tuesdays. 'The Free Rent Band' is playing tonight."

"Oh man!" Marge squealed. "I love that band. I wish I were going with you."

"What time to you get off, Marge?" Craig asked with a grin.

"Unfortunately, not until late, and I can't afford to fake being sick. I need the job," she said while vigorously snapping a wad of bubble gum that appeared to be even pinker than the movie set for "Barbie."

"Bummer," said Craig. "Do you know where we can get some good cigars?"

"Yes. There are a number of places. I've heard my regulars talk about 'Fidel's.' I think it's on Pennsylvania Ave. There's also 'The Outlaw Cigar Company,' but I'm not sure where it is. I guess you can Google it."

"Thanks, Marge. And thanks for the great service," Craig said, smiling expansively.

"It's my pleasure," Marge purred.

Locking onto her eyes, Craig asked, "Do you work here full-time, Marge?"

"Pretty much. I also waitress during lunch service at a number of places in town."

"Sounds like you're very busy," Craig observed. "Do you ever get any time off?"

Sighing, her voice and countenance suddenly reflecting a soul-wrenching weariness, Marge replied, "Not much. There was a time when the sky was the limit. I married my high school sweetheart. Neither of us went to college, but he had planned to follow in his father's footsteps and work in the stockyards. It wasn't a dream job but was steady and provided decent pay and benefits. Unfortunately, the stockyards closed for good in 1991. He ended up working a number of manual labor jobs. We weren't rich by any means, but with two incomes, we were able to get by and save a little money for a house. We dreamed of raising a family, but that blew up when he was injured at work, got hooked on pain meds, and ultimately died of a heroin overdose. I've struggled to make ends meet ever since."

Stunned by Marge's comments, Craig said, "I'm so sorry to hear that, Marge. Please excuse me if I got too personal."

"It's okay," Marge said, biting her lip. "Life goes on."

With that, Marge gathered herself and pressed on to other customers with her cheerful mask back on full display.

Feeling badly that he had unintentionally ripped the scab off a wound that wouldn't heal, Craig turned to Steve and said, "That was unfortunate. I was just trying to make conversation."

"Don't feel bad, Craig. She wouldn't have told you if she hadn't wanted to," Steve said.

"I guess you're right," Craig replied. "Still…"

Leaning back as he savored his last rib while glancing at Marge as she hustled from table to table, Craig regained his composure and enthused, "The concierge was right about this place—delicious. The barbeque is the best I've ever had. And this beer is really good too. I always make a point of trying the local craft beers."

"I'm getting to like craft beers," Steve said. "But my 'house beer' is Bud Light, which of course, originated here in Missouri. I'm not a beer snob like you," he joked.

"I'm surprised you're not boycotting Bud Light or shooting it up like Kid Rock because Bud Light did an ad with a 'trans' influencer," Craig teased.

"And waste all that beer?" Steve snickered. "No way."

"I wouldn't pour a Bud on the lawn in my backyard," Craig said as he laughed and punched Steve on the shoulder. "It tastes like 'panther piss.'"

"Do you do a lot of sampling of cat piss?" Steve needled. "And what backyard would that be in Manhattan?"

"I'm speaking figuratively." Craig chuckled.

Taking a sip of his beer, Steve said, "I have a question for you, Craig. Would you really have had Marge join us?"

"Maybe. She seems like a lot of fun—even if a little sad."

"She doesn't strike me as what I imagine to be your type," Steve said.

"She isn't," Craig replied. "But a little flirting is always fun. I noticed you didn't say a thing."

"I guess I froze because I was scared you were serious."

"Loosen up, Bro. We're on a pleasure cruise. It's okay to flirt a bit and maybe even get a little action. Tammy isn't here. Speaking of Tammy, I only met her for a few minutes, but my quick impression is that she's very smart."

"Yeah. She's smart—maybe too smart," Steve sighed.

"How can she be too smart?" Craig asked. "To me, the sexiest part of any woman is her brain."

"Maybe," Steve said. "But there's a thin line between 'smart' and 'smart ass.' You tell me: was her comment about the Red Shark smart or smart ass?"

"I thought it was terrific—very astute."

"Tammy isn't a snob, but can definitely get under your skin. She belongs to both a poetry group and a book club. They meet every other week with the participants hosting in their homes. I make a point of not being there when it's our house. I can't tell you how many times I've heard her rant about the lack of reading among Americans. I can even quote the statistics: thirty-three percent of high school graduates never read another book the rest of their lives; forty-two percent of college grads never read another book after college; eighty percent of American families didn't buy or read a book last year; on and on— ad nauseam. She's been bugging me about reading for years."

"I hadn't heard those statistics before," Craig said. "I think Tammy's concern is valid. My mother always told me that all bigotry is based on ignorance. I happen to agree. Books expose a person to worlds and ideas outside their own experience."

"I concede that Tammy's point is valid," Steve said. "Reading not only educates about the broader world but also makes people more likely to understand the emotions of others. But, damn—enough already."

"I think Tammy is right on. For Christ's sake, Steve, you're a college professor and a role model to your kids. It's all in the way you look at it. It sounds to me like Tammy is all for you."

Laughing, Steve said, "Wait a minute. Are you, a two-time loser, giving me advice about marriage? Besides, as a historian, I've already read about and am well-versed in my subject matter."

"But isn't it essential in your courses to know current events and thinking to make history relevant. I always understood that the present informs the past and the past informs the present and future. As to being a two-time loser, I concede your point," Craig said while toasting Steve and laughing.

"Okay, 'Tammy,' I give up," Steve said sarcastically. Finishing his beer and suggesting to Craig that they get another round, he said, "As to women, I would say you're very successful. They were always throwing themselves at you in college, including the other-worldly Sophia Caputo."

"For all we know, Sophia could weigh two hundred pounds at this point," Craig laughed as he caught Marge's eye and signaled for two more beers.

Chuckling, Steve said, "I'd be willing to bet that Sophia is still drop-dead gorgeous. Besides, I'm pretty sure the 'Woke Police' would arrest you for 'body shaming' if they overheard your comment."

"Fair enough," Craig conceded.

Marge quickly retrieved the drafts and, ignoring Steve as if he were a piece of furniture, bent down to serve Craig while providing him the bonus of a provocative sight line. As their eyes met, it was pretty clear to Craig that Marge's serving technique was practiced and the unbuttoned top of her blouse no accident.

Craig smiled from ear to ear appreciatively as he thanked her. Marge smiled back coquettishly before pivoting and moving on to help other customers.

"Before we get into a discussion of women in general—which is tough to do with Marge hovering nearby—let me ask you a question. Have you taken Tammy's advice about reading?"

"Sort of. I've recently finished two books. One was an excellent non-fiction book on Lincoln, and the other was a rereading of *The Great Gatsby*, which I first read in high school. I must admit that I was surprised by *Gatsby*. It made me wonder if I'd really read it the first time around. It's amazing how adding a few years gives you both perspective and perception. I actually highlighted a number of passages that struck me and brought the book with me so that I can think about those passages during any down time we have or on an airplane if we decide to fly home."

"There won't be any down time, Bro. I don't want us to be pressed to do everything I have in mind—after all, this isn't a forced march—but there's so much to do and so little time. By the way, I would recommend you read Heather Cox Richardson's book *How the South Won the Civil War.* [vii] It's a wonderful take on how the past informs current events."

"Okay, 'Tammy,'" Steve said, laughing as the two of them leaned back in their chairs and admired Marge, who remained attentive, glancing back at them while serving other customers.

"I did a little research on Missouri politics before coming," Craig said. "What does Tammy think about all this book burning?"

"What book burning?" Steve asked.

"Okay," Craig replied. "It's not book burning per se, but it might as well be. My understanding is that Missouri has criminalized displaying certain books in libraries."

"Oh—you mean pornographic books," Steve said.

"Like what, for example?" Craig challenged.

"Books like Toni Morrison's *Beloved* that mention rape, incest, and infanticide. Why wouldn't we want to keep those kinds of books away from kids? If a parent wants their child to read a particular book, that's their individual choice, but those books shouldn't be made available in schools."

"How about the Bible?" Craig asked. "It mentions not only rape, incest, and infanticide, but also bestiality, prostitution, fellatio, and dildos, among other things."

"The Bible is sacred," Steve shot back. "Besides, I don't remember those references."

"You need to learn your Bible a little bit better, Steve. Read about the Rape of Dinah in Genesis and Lot's daughters getting him drunk to have sex with him." [viii]

Craig continued, "Did you know that for years the most banned book in America was *Nineteen Eighty-Four* by George Orwell? How ironically 'Orwellian.' Books like Harper Lee's *To Kill a Mockingbird*, Anne Frank's *The Diary of a Young Girl*, and JK Rowling's *Harry Potter* series, have been banned by various school districts. *Beloved,* which you just mentioned, won the Pulitzer Prize for Fiction. My God, Steve, these are some of the most highly regarded books of all time and are serious works of art—some with important historical context. Furthermore, by criminalizing the display of so-called objectionable books, as Missouri has done, there's a chilling effect. As I understand it, over three hundred books have been removed from libraries. And it doesn't stop there. Did you read how a school principal in Florida was fired because she showed a picture of Michelangelo's marble masterpiece 'David' in an art history class and at least one parent deemed the sculpture pornographic?"

"I'm not defending book bans, Craig. And I'm pretty certain Tammy wouldn't either. But don't be a hypocrite. Did you see the story about Stanford law students—yes, law students who should know better—shouting down a conservative judge during a talk at the law school and the Stanford administrator present rising not to defend the judge's right to talk but rather to defend the disruptive behavior of the students? And how about the professor who said it would be far more admirable to 'kill' the speaker than protest?"

"I don't condone either," Craig said. "The Stanford administrator was put on leave, and the Wayne State professor was suspended after his outrageous comments. He was also referred to the police by the University—which is appropriate. I can understand your analogy, but that's not book burning."

Getting agitated, Steve shot back, "Really? Then how about the 'Woke' crowd trying to rewrite books like Roald Dahl's *Charlie and the Chocolate Factory* to remove potentially offensive language by substituting 'enormous' for 'enormously fat' or making characters gender neutral? They've also tried to ban or sanitize *The Adventures of Tom Sawyer* and *Adventures of Huckleberry Finn* by Mark

Twain, a local hero from Hannibal, Missouri, because the books are considered racist and the 'N' word is used. I don't condone the use of the 'N' word, but, as you mentioned, books like that provides important historical context. And you need to research your arguments more fully. It's 'progressive' elites rather than conservatives behind the banning of *To Kill a Mockingbird*."

Raising his voice, Craig countered, "How about Florida banning so-called 'critical race theory' and substituting a history that suggests that slaves benefited from slavery by learning useful skills? The second amendment is absolute in the minds of your crowd, but the first amendment isn't?"

Steve leaned back, took a sip of his beer, and consciously deescalating, said softly, "I think you and I could come to common ground on all of these issues, Craig."

Relaxing in his seat and smiling, Craig responded in kind: "I agree, Bro. The extremists appear to be winning on each side of these 'culture' arguments rather than the moderate middle. It's too bad the general public can't make these decisions, or we move to 'ranked-choice' voting to elect moderates. As you mentioned earlier, we've seen what happens when measures like extreme abortion bans are defeated time and again in referenda."

"Amen," Steve said. Chuckling, he quipped, "And my use of the word 'Amen' isn't a proclamation of the 'Christian Nation.'"

Laughing and pausing to take a sip of his beer, Craig said, "Okay. Enough of this topic. We're here to have fun—not solve the world's problems. Let's pick up our earlier discussion about women. I didn't say I haven't been with lots of women. After a while, it became a 'beige blur.' I've just been unsuccessful in finding the right partner. My first marriage was all about lust. I disregarded my mother's advice about great sex not being able to sustain you long term. I was 'head-over-heels' and thought I knew best."

"Your mother talked to you about sex?" Steve asked, his mouth agape in mock disbelief. "My mother would have never broached that subject."

"We had different upbringings, Steve. Manhattan and Missouri are from different galaxies."

Craig continued, "I was very careful with my second marriage. Looks and sex were still important, but I was mature enough at that point to know my best chance would be with a smart, accomplished woman. She was both— running an art gallery in Chelsea."

"So what happened?"

"You never met her because neither of us wanted a big wedding. For both of my marriages, we simply went to a JP. In any event, my second wife's real name turned out to be 'Plaintiff.'"

"I'm not sure I'm following you," Steve said as he took a long drink of his beer.

"Because I was in my mid-thirties the second time around, I had already made lots of money and insisted on a pre-nuptial agreement."

"Woah!" Steve blurted out, accidentally spraying beer spittle in Craig's direction. Wiping his mouth with the back of his hand, he said, "I don't think I would have the guts to ask that of a woman. It's like announcing: 'I love you—but I'm hedging my bets.'"

"I agree it doesn't sound very romantic, and I can see how a prospective partner might be put off. However, having been burned once, I was simply being pragmatic—and, I guess, a little defensive."

"So what went wrong?"

"Just about everything," Craig replied with a pained expression. "Once the 'honeymoon' was over, I realized that she was headstrong and had to have things her way. I'm pretty headstrong myself, and yet I did my best to try and accommodate her—but after a while, all I could hear in my head when I saw her was Santana's song about changing my life to suit her whims." [ix]

"I think 'Smooth' is Santana's best," Steve said. "I hope I don't develop a earworm just thinking about the song or that line in particular with respect to Tammy. So what happened?"

"When we decided to split up, I thought, 'Thank God I have the Pre-Nup.' But she sued alleging that I had been mentally and verbally abusive as well as 'controlling,' and that she had been coerced into signing the agreement. Her lawsuit demanded an equal division of assets plus damages for pain and suffering."

"Bummer," Steve said. "What was the outcome?"

"Her lawyer was a bastard—probably just reflecting the demands of his client. The litigation was public and grist for the gossip mills—which was not great for business or my social life. The initial complaint was followed by an unending series of motions, interrogatories, depositions, subpoenas, and the like—and I was being forced by the Court to pay her lawyer's fees. Clearly, there was no incentive for them to back off, and it became overwhelming. I just wanted out and finally agreed to a settlement that upped the Pre-Nup by four million dollars."

"Four million dollars!" Steve gasped. "My God, I don't think I'll make that much in my entire life, but for you, it was just minor inconvenience."

"It was more than a minor inconvenience, Steve. Most importantly, it has soured my view when it comes to prospective partners. I've dated a lot—and there are plenty of women who want a decent-looking guy in his forties with an expansive net worth—but I have trouble with 'trust' issues at this point and can't help wondering if they're gold diggers or chameleons. If I don't take the plunge again, I worry what will happen as I get older. Will those willing women fade away? Will I be alone? Will I ever have a family? Do I care?"

"I don't know what to say, Craig. Tammy and I have our problems, like all married couples, but I know she wouldn't cheat on me and wouldn't try to take me to the cleaners if we decided to call it quits. At least I don't think so. It's just that we're in a rut."

"Even though I'm a two-time loser, I again suggest you ask yourself to consider whether Tammy is nagging you or trying to help. It's all about perspective—something you just acknowledged grows with experience."

"I'm not sure nagging and trying to help are mutually exclusive thoughts," Steve retorted.

"Fair enough," Craig said as he toasted Steve and drained his beer.

As they settled up, Craig again thanked Marge for a special evening. In addition to exchanging smiles, she slipped him a paper napkin on which she had written down her name and phone number.

***

The concierge had told the guys that "Knuckleheads Saloon" is a "biker bar" with multiple stages for live music running the gamut from Elvis tributes to rock, blues, country, reggae, and gospel.

Craig and Steve were blown away as soon as they entered the Saloon. It's the original venue of the multi-stage complex with a "honky-tonk" feel famous for sponsoring open jam sessions on weekend days where amateurs can join in with pros. It has hosted musicians like Leon Russell, Tower of Power, and many others. The walls are covered with pictures of musicians who have played there, and the place oozes music.

"I love joints like this," Craig enthused as they inhaled the surroundings. "I was in Pensacola for business recently, and my host took me to a place in Orange Beach, Alabama, called the 'Flora-Bama Beach Bar.' It's forty-five minutes west of Pensacola, just beyond the Florida panhandle, right on the Gulf. It's part of the 'Redneck

Riviera.' As a card-carrying redneck, I assume you know the area, Steve," he said with a smirk.

Playfully punching Craig on the shoulder, Steve responded, "I know of it but have never been."

"Before following my friend into the bar, I paused to take in the brilliant white sand beaches. They really pop in the sun framed by the blue waters of the Gulf. I was momentarily transported to a fairyland hearing Jimmy Buffett's cover of the old standard 'Stars Fell on Alabama' and the magical scene he painted of he and his lover—just the two of them—kissing while illuminated by white all around them." [x]

"Wait a minute," Steve said. "That song was about a meteor shower."

"I know—but for just an instant, I was there—it was heavenly—just like in the song. I have trouble coming up with the word or words to describe the experience."

"Is the word 'spiritual'?" Steve asked. "Before you even say it, let me be clear that I'm not talking religion."

"Maybe. Unfortunately, as usual, reality intervened and I was shaken awake once I moved inside."

"I'm all ears," Steve said.

"The bar has live music nightly. Women strip off their bras, bare their breasts, and throw the bras up on the ceiling fans. I certainly wouldn't call that 'spiritual,'" Craig said, chuckling. "Maybe spirited, but not spiritual. And although great fun, it was certainly a step down from being enraptured."

"Yeah, but it certainly gives new meaning to being a 'fan,'" Steve chortled.

"Agreed," Craig said, laughing. "It's not something you'd experience in Manhattan. Lots of salt-of-the-earth Midwesterners and 'good ole boys' and gals cutting loose and just having a ball—no commitments necessary. But to this day, I keep having flashbacks of that moment kissing under a meteor shower—longing for it to be real."

"I hope you get there some day, Bro," Steve said.

After pausing, Steve continued, "You mentioned earlier that we're from different galaxies. How is it that a born and bred New Yorker gets off on such a scene?"

"It must be the Mizzou in me," Craig said laughing. "New Yorkers can have fun, and there are dive bars in Manhattan, but too often I find myself in upscale bars, with upscale people, overpaying for upscale drinks, and engaging in upscale repartee. Remember Billy Joel's song about not wanting to labor at skillful conversation? [xi] That's the way I feel."

"I'm a little surprised to hear that, Dude. You and I are friends, but I thought that, in general, New Yorkers and other coastal elites look down on people like Tammy and me."

"What are you talking about?" Craig protested— totally perplexed.

"Oh please. How about Hillary Clinton describing guys like me as 'deplorables,' or Barack Obama describing blue collar whites in places suffering job losses as clinging to guns, religion and hatred of 'others' who don't look like them?"

"I can't speak for either of them, but I don't feel that way. I must admit, I do wonder why blue collar whites vote against their economic interests. And by the way, you're a college professor; why would you lump yourself in with 'blue collar whites?'"

"You said it, Craig. I'm a redneck. Besides, adjunct professors are paid with a title—not real money. Perhaps you said it unwittingly, but differentiating me from blue collar whites and giving me a pass just because I have a title says it all about elitism. As to voting against our economic interests, we didn't leave the Democratic Party; it left us to cater to those 'upscale' people you mentioned—as well as aggrieved 'tribes' wallowing in identity politics," Steve said. "All this 'wokeness' nonsense that penalizes white males like me is unbearable."

"But it isn't a zero sum game, Steve. A rising tide raises all boats."

"Sounds nice theoretically, but I only know what I know," Steve fired back—raising his voice. "Did you see the news about a man—who happened to be white— having an offer to be superintendent of a school district in Massachusetts rescinded because he addressed two of the School Committee members as 'ladies' in an email and they regarded the reference as a 'microaggession?' Sounds more like a 'falling tide' to me."

"I think we each need a drink," Craig said. "Let's hit the bar after we tour the rest of the complex."

"Deal!" Steve said, eager to move on.

The "Garage" was so-named because it was originally a truck, school bus, and motor home facility, but with its transformation, it exuded a funky vibe. "The Wall," a mural painted on the front of the Garage, features departed musicians like country singer Rodney Crowell, Burton Cummings of "The Guess Who," as well as others. It's the largest indoor venue in the complex and can seat up to six hundred.

As they left the 'Garage,' Craig whispered to Steve, "Check out that sign. 'No Guns Allowed At Knuckleheads.'"

"Yeah. I noticed a similar sign when we first came in," Steve whispered. "My weapon is concealed, so no one is likely to see it. Besides—what can they do? Throw us out? It's not illegal."

"Okay, Bro, although I suspect others harbor those same feelings," Craig replied.

"I can live with that," Steve snickered.

"I hope we all can," Craig sighed.

The "Gospel Lounge" is the most intimate stage, seating no more than seventy-five. Artists reportedly love performing there because of the easy interaction with the crowd.

The outdoor stage has seating capacity of hundreds with a converted caboose to one side as a VIP seating area. There are great sightlines and views of the Kansas City sky. A train track runs nearby. Local legend has it that one night, singer-songwriter Joe Ely was performing his song, "Boxcar," when a train came by, blowing its whistle as if on cue, with Ely declaring that he had waited twenty years for the train to pass and sound off at the perfect time.

After touring the complex, the two of them headed for the bar in the saloon.

Upon entering, Craig marveled at the stage, the second largest indoor music venue, which he noted has an aura that you can almost smell, taste and feel.

"I think your observation about 'smell' is right on," Steve said. "The overhead fans are nice, but the lack of AC in these ninety degree temperatures should create a real aroma once the bar gets crowded."

As Steve and he grabbed a couple of bar stools, Craig asked the bartender, whose name was Ben, "What's the most famous Kansas City drink?"

Without hesitation, Ben, who sported an impressive handlebar mustache that offset his rapidly receding hairline, answered emphatically, "Kansas City Ice Water."

"Okay. I'll bite," Craig said. "What's 'Kansas City Ice Water?'"

"It's a delightful concoction consisting of gin, vodka, triple sec, lime juice, and a lemon-flavored carbonated beverage served over lots of ice."

Pausing, Ben added, "Although not specific to Kansas City, there's also the 'Missouri Mule,' which was named after native son, President Harry Truman. There are various recipes, but bourbon is key. Bourbon was Truman's drink of choice. He apparently had a 'wee dram' each day after his two mile walk. We add applejack, compari, triple sec, and lemon juice."

"Is it named 'mule' because President Truman was so stubborn?" Craig asked.

Laughing as he twisted one end of his mustache and then the other, Ben said, "One might think that, but believe it or not, the 'mule' is the State animal of Missouri and has a hell of a kick."

"Good to see that the government spends its time on such weighty matters," Craig said while laughing. "What do you think, Steve, shall we have one of each?"

"I'm game," Steve replied.

Alternating between their two drinks, Craig and Steve kicked back and lit up cigars as the crowd began to trickle in and the band set up. The cigars were "Ashton Classics," featuring a golden-blonde "Connecticut Shade" wrapper leaf embracing a premium aged inner of Dominican tobaccos blended by cigar-making legend Carlito Fuente. The manager at "Fidel's" they met with was a cigar "sommelier" who, like his wine counterparts, talked a lot about "terroir" and rhapsodized about the "Classic," exhibiting silky notes of cashews, cedar, coffee, and a touch of signature Dominican spices.

"We hear a lot about Cuban, Dominican, and Nicaraguan cigar tobaccos," Craig said. "But did you know that the best cigars are wrapped with a tobacco leaf from the Connecticut River Valley? There are three types of leaf: 'Shade,' 'Broadleaf,' and a minor type known as 'Havana.' Even Cuban cigars makers prefer locally grown Connecticut leaf wrappers because they offer a refined flavor and hint of sweetness not matched by other tobacco."

"I had no idea," Steve said while savoring his cigar.

"On my way to skiing, I drive by these long barns in Connecticut that are actually 'tobacco sheds,' but never knew what they were. One day, as I was driving north at the beginning of the ski season, I observed quite a bit of activity at one shed and stopped in to find out what was going on. Apparently, you have to 'air-cure' tobacco by hanging the leaves in well-ventilated sheds for four to eight weeks. The 'Shades' are harvested in mid-October, but the 'Broadleafs' are harvested as late as mid-November. It was the Broadleafs that were being cured."

"News to me." Steve said. "I learn something every day."

"I'm convinced that intellectual curiosity and learning new things is a key to happiness, which is why reading is so important," Craig said as he leaned back on his bar stool and took a pull on his cigar, allowing the smoke to swirl in his mouth while drawing it to the back of his throat before exhaling through his nose. "I learned about 'pulling' on a cigar from a friend years ago. The key is to use your mouth and not your lungs."

"Thanks for the tutorial, Professor Wells," Steve said while executing his own "pull."

"By the way, Craig," Steve said, tongue in cheek. "Looking at this Knuckleheads cocktail napkin, I wonder if it's a candidate to be mailed to Otis."

"That's the spirit, Bro. It's probably not exotic enough to add to Otis's collection, but it's a good thought," Craig said laughing. "Maybe you could join me in the messaging. A second set of handwriting would probably throw Otis for a loop."

"Or make him paranoid." Steve chuckled.

When Ben returned to refresh their drinks, Craig asked how many nights a week he bartended at Knuckleheads.

"As many nights as I can get," Ben replied. "It's usually at least five nights. I also work as a real estate agent during the days."

"When do you sleep?" Craig asked.

"When I can," Ben replied, chuckling.

"Do you like bartending?" Craig asked.

"It's okay. The tip money is great, and I enjoy the music. Having said that, sometimes the amps are so loud I think I'll need hearing aids by the time I'm forty." Ben laughed. "And I think all this smoke in the bar, mixed with the heat and humidity, is making me lose my hair," he joked.

"So why do you keep at it?" Craig asked. "There are other jobs out there."

"It works out time-wise to supplement my day job. Real estate commissions are great, but it's a boom or bust business. That's okay for those fortunate enough to have a spouse with a steady income, but my fiancée and I want to buy a home and raise a family with her as a stay-at-home mom. We think it's the right thing to do for the kids, but it's like that great line in the song 'Spike' by Tom Petty about the future not being as rosy as it once was." [xii]

"What do you mean by that?" Steve asked.

"I'll hold my tongue," Ben said. "My mom always said if you want to remain friends with someone, avoid discussions about politics and religion. I think it's good advice that jibes with my job as a bartender. All I'll say is that I wish it were a little easier."

"Good luck to you," Steve said while he and Craig toasted Ben.

As Craig rose to shake Ben's hand, he palmed a one-hundred-dollar tip to Ben, whispering, "This is for you; not for a tip pot."

"Thanks guys. God bless you," Ben said as he discreetly slipped the Benjamin into his pocket.

The crowd filled out and revved up for the show with drinks and spirited conversation that soon pulsated throughout the saloon. Neither Craig nor Steve had heard of "The Free Rent Band" before but eagerly joined in the festive mood as the band began to play. The heat of the crowd—unmitigated by AC—cranked up the temperature inside, but Craig and Steve threw caution to the wind and decided "what the hell" as they joined in the sweaty celebration.

Feeling the energy of the crowd, the two of them stood with other patrons swaying rhythmically as they kept time with the music lifting them into a human "murmuration" as they belted out words from the refrain in the band's song "Speakeasy" about liquor and cigars on their breath.

During intermission, a local band took the stage and played several of their original songs. A young woman with spiked blue hair and a prominent nose ring rushed the stage and threw liquid from a red solo cup in the face of the lead singer while live streaming. Shocked and not knowing what the liquid was, the band came to an abrupt halt. "It's just water," the girl shouted as she continued to live stream before jumping from the stage, quickly surrounded by several girlfriends who greeted her like a "star" as they melted into the audience.

"What an inconsiderate asshole," Steve bellowed.

"Pretty selfish," Craig concurred.

After taking a minute to gather themselves, the band resumed without further interruption.

Toward the end of the concert—after The Free Rent Band had returned to complete their set—the blue-haired girl and her friends passed by the bar. Steve shocked Craig by pouring a glass of beer on her head.

"What in the fuck do you think you're doing?" she protested angrily.

Steve laughed and said, "Just returning the favor. I would have live streamed it if I knew how."

"Fuck you!" the girl screamed as her face contorted with hatred. She spit in Steve's face and stormed out with her acolytes in close pursuit.

"Wow!" Craig said to Steve. "I didn't see that coming. I guess the college professor has some moxie after all."

Laughing, Steve said, "Seeing her toss the contents of that red solo cup, I couldn't help but think of the 'beer pong' games we played in college and just took it from there."

"What would Tammy have to say about that?" Craig teased.

"What Tammy doesn't know won't hurt her," Steve chortled.

***

But for the water tossing incident and near sauna-like conditions, the concert was terrific. Craig and Steve were so jacked up at the end that they were reluctant to call it a night even though they had a long drive to Boulder, Colorado, the next day. As for Steve, his apprehension about spending time with the über-successful Craig had flown out the window with his spontaneous dousing of the spotlight-seeking interloper. It was as if he and Craig had been together the day before yesterday and were both nineteen again—both beautiful—without a care in the world—facing only boundless possibilities ahead.

The two of them drifted into a speakeasy Ben had recommended half a block from their hotel.

Feeling the gush of cool air that almost took their breath away, Craig said, "Thank God for AC."

Steve readily agreed, mentioning the torture he and Tammy were going through without.

"But there's no climate change, is there?" Craig taunted.

Steve ignored the comment and ordered bourbon on the rocks for the two of them.

"To Harry Truman," Steve offered as he toasted Craig.

"To Harry Truman," Craig responded.

As they sipped their bourbons and smoked cigars winding down after the concert at Knuckleheads, Steve suddenly stiffened. He put a twenty on the bar to pay for their drinks and whispered, "Let's get out of here—right now."

Craig protested, "What? Why?"

"Don't ask questions. Just follow me."

As they exited the speakeasy, Craig asked, "What in the hell is going on?"

Steve was resolute, suddenly sober, and his face an ashen gray. "Just walk quickly. I'll explain when we get to our hotel."

Entering the room and latching the deadbolt, Steve was clearly shaken.

"You look like you saw a ghost," Craig said.

"No—just two groups of guys getting into an argument at the end of the bar. It was getting more and more heated. So much for 'speaking easy.' I don't know if you noticed, but each of them had open carry weapons. When one of them pushed another, my sixth sense told me we needed to get out of there immediately."

"My God!" Craig exclaimed. "I was oblivious."

Pausing for a minute, Craig observed: "Your reaction sounds like the 'hyper-vigilance' that vets talk about when returning from combat with PTSD. Always alert; always anxious. Is that what the world of open and concealed carry means for us now, with stress hormones flooding our systems at all times? That isn't a way to live."

"Like it or not, it's the new reality," Steve replied.

"It's not a world I want to live in," Craig said.

After both calmed down, Craig asked, "Steve, have you called Tammy to let her know we arrived safely?"

"I texted her," Steve said.

"Call her, Steve. 'The last call of the day.' It's meaningful."

"Good night, Craig," Steve said.

Chapter 3
"Jayhawks" and "Buffaloes"

"It's soooo early," Steve groaned. "Christ—we're on vacation. Once we get to Las Vegas, I don't want to get up before noon."

"Okay. But we have a long drive today," Craig coaxed. "GPS says it will be around nine hours, but we'll make it shorter by ignoring speed limits. I filled the cooler with fresh ice from the hotel's ice machine and box lunches the hotel made for us, as well as beer left over from yesterday. We don't have to stop except to answer calls of nature. I'm hoping we can make it to the University of Colorado in Boulder by late afternoon. I've been in touch with the Athletic Department, and they've agreed to let us tour the basketball arena if we get there before five."

"Ah," Steve said. "Reliving the glory days, huh? If I recall correctly, it was there where you scored over forty points one game."

"I confess. That arena and the Buffaloes were always good to me."

"Why don't we visit the University of Kansas on the way?" Steve taunted. "Lawrence is right off I-70 West, only forty-five minutes from here."

"No thanks," Craig said while laughing. "That place was my house of horrors. They kicked our asses every year."

"I remember only too well," Steve said. "Okay, let's hit the road. You take the first shift while I wake up."

The two of them piled into the Red Shark, pulled the car onto the interstate shortly after seven in the morning, and headed west.

They barely spoke for the first half hour as Steve slumbered. As they approached Lawrence, he finally came up for air and asked, "Do you know where the name 'Lawrence' came from?"

"Not a clue," Craig responded.

"It was named after an abolitionist from Ipswich, Massachusetts, named Amos Lawrence. Didn't you ever wonder why the main drag in Lawrence is named 'Massachusetts Street?'"

"Nope. Never gave it a thought," Craig replied.

"When Kansas was being admitted to the Union, there were open hostilities over whether Kansas would become a 'Slave State,' like Missouri, or a 'Free State.' It got so bad that a congressman from South Carolina attacked Senator Charles Sumner from Massachusetts on the Senate floor and nearly beat him to death with a steel-topped cane." [xiii]

"Seriously?" Craig gasped. "And I thought the country was divided today."

"Yeah," Steve replied. "Of course the divisions back then were so bad it led to the Civil War. Hopefully, we won't lose our minds and go off the deep end again."

"From your lips to God's ears. So what happened? I don't recall whether Kansas became a free state or a slave state."

The 'Free Staters' ultimately prevailed, but only because abolitionists from New England and other Northern States settled here in numbers with the express purpose of keeping Kansas free." [xiv]

"I had no idea," Craig said. "I guess Senator Sumner got his revenge."

"I hadn't thought of that way, but I guess you're right," Steve said.

Steve continued, "Amos Lawrence donated a lot of money so that the University of Kansas would be located in Lawrence. You might also be interested to know that the first basketball coach of Kansas was the famous James Naismith, who invented the game of basketball in Massachusetts, where the 'Naismith Basketball Hall of Fame' is located. As it turns out, he's the only losing coach in Kansas history."

"Damn." Craig laughed. "Why couldn't he have coached while we were playing?"

"So why are the University of Kansas teams called the 'Jayhawks?'" Craig asked.

"I suspect that most people have forgotten that the origin of the name goes back to the Civil War, where the 'Jayhawkers' fought on the side of the Free Staters and Quantrill's Raiders fought on the side of the South. They were both ruthless, with Quantrill's Raiders killing scores of civilians and burning Lawrence to the ground."

"I must admit, Steve, I was ignorant as to any of this history when we traveled to Lawrence as college kids. Like your rereading of *The Great Gatsby*, you've given me a completely different perspective now—twenty-five years later. If we drive back, I'd like to make time to visit Lawrence."

"Sounds like a plan," Steve agreed.

"I think it's time for an eye-opener," Craig said. "How about you?"

"Sounds good," Steve replied as he reached into the cooler and retrieved a couple of beers.

As they drove on, Craig asked, "So how did you meet Tammy?"

"I didn't fuss with church while we were in college—except when I was home at Christmas, Easter, and during the summer. I just wanted to sleep in Sunday mornings after partying every Saturday night."

"'Sleep in," Craig scowled. "Wouldn't 'sleep it off' be more accurate?"

"Fair enough," Steve said, laughing. "In any event, once I graduated, I wasn't sure what I wanted to do and ended up living with my parents for a bit while entering the management training track at The Bank of Missouri. Not wanting to disappoint my Mom and Dad, I just fell back into old patterns, including going to church and church-sponsored activities like cleaning up litter at parks, church picnics, and volunteering at the church food pantry. Tammy had moved to Columbia from Iowa while I was in college. I didn't know her but happened to get assigned to her team at a church-sponsored scavenger hunt one evening. My first thought was how corny and boring that would be. It turned out to be a blast. Someone had given a lot of thought to very clever clues, and Tammy stood out as very quick with an answer, very funny, and a great team player. I just took a shine to her, and one thing led to another."

"So how did she take to you playing in a band?"

"She likes rock and roll and thought it was cool—although she never approved of the tattoos."

"Did Tammy ever make the connection between the pineal gland tattoo and pineal gland extract?"

"I don't think so. Thank God or she would have harassed me mercilessly until it was removed."

"So what caused you to leave the management track at the bank and move to Mizzou?" Craig asked.

"I hated management but loved history. It was my major in college. When a friend tipped me about a lecturer's position opening up at Mizzou, I jumped at it. I was surprised—but elated—when I got the position. The fact that I was a 'legacy' helped, but, of course, I was required to enhance my academic credentials by simultaneously getting a Master's Degree in history. That wasn't a problem; in fact, I enjoyed it. I was strongly advised to pursue a Ph.D. but never followed through."

"Not yet, Steve. It's never too late," Craig replied. "It sounds like both Tammy and the position at Mizzou are a perfect fit."

"Yeah—in theory," Steve responded.

After a pause where neither was eager to pursue that line of thinking further, Steve asked, "And how about you,

Craig? How did you end up with your own private equity firm?"

"My father was big in wealth management in Manhattan. He got me a job at Goldman Sachs. I learned the ropes there. Two colleagues and I decided to take the leap and launch the private equity firm. My Dad was very helpful in getting us our first set of investors—as were my partners' connections. That was key because you can't attract investments without a track record and you can't develop a track record without investments. I like to think of myself as a 'self-made' man but know in my heart that without a helping hand, hell, I might have been in a management training program at a local bank."

Realizing that his quip about the bank might hurt, Craig quickly added, "No offense intended."

"None taken," Steve replied. "In fact, your comment is right on. But don't sell yourself short. You had the smarts and drive to make it happen."

"Thanks, Bro. Let's just say that I recognize that I'm very privileged to be where I am in the financial world. From time to time, I think about all those who aren't so fortunate."

Twenty-five minutes later, as they neared Topeka, Craig observed, "I'm a little surprised by Kansas. It produces more wheat than any other state and is known as the 'Sunflower State.' As I focus on it now, a thousand years after our mindless bus rides to the University of Kansas and Kansas State to play basketball, this area doesn't look any different than Missouri."

"Patience, my friend," Steve counseled. "The change will come. It really becomes dramatic closer to Kansas State."

After taking a swig of a fresh beer, Steve asked, "In addition to being the state capital, do you know what else Topeka is famous for?"

"Once again, I have no idea. My God—I'm glad we're not playing 'Trivial Pursuit' with the category being 'History' or 'Geography.' I'd look like a blithering idiot."

"You are a blithering idiot," Steve said laughing, "at least as to history. I think you'd need a remedial history course before you could get into my introductory freshman course at Mizzou."

Steve continued, "'Brown vs. The Board of Education,' which as you know eliminated segregation in schools, came from here. Because we shorten everything, people forget that the actual lawsuit was named 'Brown vs. The Board of Education of Topeka.'

"And yet we still haven't lived out our creed: 'all men are created equal,'" Craig lamented.

"But look how far we've come," Steve said. "Kansas played pivotal roles in eliminating slavery and then eliminating segregation. Easterners think that they're the center of the universe and give Middle Americans little credit for important historical events or for progress."

"Man. Do all Midwesterners have inferiority complexes?" Craig asked.

"I don't have an inferiority complex," Steve protested. "I think coastal elites have a superiority complex and speak down to us, which is part of the reason we recoil reflexively at dictates from so-called 'experts.' I just feel duty-bound to point out that meaningful history happens here too."

"Okay," Craig said. "I know and appreciate that."

"I believe you, Bro, but I think you're the exception to the rule. Not many coastal elites went to Mizzou."

"Man, I need another beer," Craig said. Cracking open a can that Steve had retrieved and taking a slug, he said, "I'm curious. You just bragged about 'progress' on social justice issues, but aren't you the same guy complaining about discrimination against white men? The Supreme Court just ruled against affirmative action."

"In my case, I think the discrimination is real. As to the Supreme Court decision, it applied to student admissions at universities. It may be applied more universally down the line—in fact, I just read that law firms are now in the crosshairs—but diversity is now a core value of institutions of higher learning, and with the widespread adoption of DEI programs, they'll find a way. You might be surprised to hear that I'm in favor of diversity generally—but that includes diversity of thought and other values and not just knee jerk affirmative action for certain aggrieved tribes. Unfortunately, there are only so many tenured professorships out there, so it becomes a zero-sum game."

"Steve, this may be hurtful to hear, but I'm going to say it anyway because, like your wife, I'm in your corner. You seem only mildly interested in reading— prompted by Tammy. Have you published any research papers in your field or at least considered publishing—each of which would require compiling extensive bibliographies?"

"No," Steve said sheepishly.

"Have you thought about developing a podcast or a course people can access on 'YouTube' like Timothy Snyder of Yale? I've been watching his course on the making of modern Ukraine, and it's fascinating."

"I'm not familiar with Snyder's course," Steve said.

"It's great fun and incredibly informative. Check it out when you get a chance. You were clearly energized telling me about Lawrence and Topeka. You could channel that same energy into an online course on Midwestern history."

"I'm not sure how I would go about that," Steve said, his voice fading.

"How about speaking to the folks at Mizzou? There must be someone there who can advise you. Or you could try and talk to Snyder directly. I'll bet he'd be willing to share some insights."

"Maybe," Steve muttered.

"How about securing a grant to explore any number of ideas? I'm sure there are grant-writing folks at Mizzou who could help."

"What would I do with a grant?" Steve responded—his voice barely above what was turning into a low growl.

"How about advancing innovative teaching methods? Or developing measurement tools to see if students are actually learning how to think about history and how it relates to current events rather than simply regurgitating facts they'll forget in a few years?"

There was no response from Steve as he grew quiet, sucking his beer dry before chucking the empty to the side of the road.

"Have you approached the young African-American woman who heads your department? She was a student more recently than you and may be brimming with fresh ideas. How about colleagues? Do you go to educational conferences? Do you reach out to counterparts in history departments in other universities to explore collaborations? I'm not a professor, but I know all of that is important for advancement in academia."

"I'm not the self-starter you are," Steve replied defensively.

"The whole world goes round based on relationships. You were a great teammate, Bro. Surely those interpersonal skills translate. Just a few minutes ago, you were animated relating those vignettes about Lawrence and Topeka to me and seemed genuinely excited. I was mesmerized. Don't blame others for failures and roadblocks. Look at yourself and find a way. And get your Ph.D."

Reacting as if he had swallowed a large dose of cod liver oil, Steve finally blurted out, "I need another beer. Can you reach the cooler? It's shifted to your side of the car."

"Sure, Steve. Sure."

***

As they drove on, the great eastern hardwood forest began to thin out and the prairie slowly emerged. Soon, the vast fields of wheat for which Kansas is famous, as well as fields of sunflower with the flowerheads all turned in worship to the 'Sun God,' appeared and went on endlessly.

"I don't think I'll ever hear the song 'America the Beautiful' again without these images of 'amber waves of grain' popping up in my mind," Craig marveled. "What can you tell me about the small patches of land not cultivated for farming? By any chance are they remnants of the tallgrass prairie that I've heard so much about?"

Taking a long drink of his fresh beer, Steve said, "They are. At one time, the tallgrass prairie covered one hundred-seventy million acres of North America, supporting the endless herds of bison. Today, less than four percent of the tallgrass remains, including in the eleven thousand acre 'Tallgrass Prairie National Preserve' in Chase County, Kansas."

As he listened, Craig remembered seeing the movie *Dances With Wolves* and the "God-shots" featuring an endless sea of grass swaying in the breeze like waves on an ocean. [xv] The thought was both inspiring and depressing at the same time. While he was glad to hear about the tall grass preserve in Chase County, he couldn't help but think about, and mention to Steve, Joni Mitchell's song lamenting destroying the beauty of the natural world and putting all the trees in a tree museum. [xvi]

As they approached the exit for Manhattan, Kansas, Craig said, "Okay. I never questioned why the main drag in Lawrence is 'Massachusetts Street.' I guess I had the same lack of curiosity when we used to play Kansas State. Why is the town called 'Manhattan?'"

"Ah," Steve said, awakening from a brief introspective stupor contemplating his academic career. "'The Little Apple.' Like Lawrence, the town was settled by abolitionists from New England headed by a teacher named Isaac Goodnow and was initially named 'Boston.' That changed when a paddle steamer named the 'Hartford' ran aground in the Kansas River near the settlement. The passengers, who were from Ohio, were part of the 'Cincinnati Manhattan Company' and had originally planned to settle twenty miles upstream at the headwaters of the Kansas River. Also 'Free-Staters,' they accepted an invitation to stay but insisted on changing the name of the town to 'Manhattan,' which was done in 1857."

Laughing, Craig quipped, "Either the settlers had an amazing lack of imagination in naming towns, or they went back to the future using an Amtrak schedule: Boston to Hartford to Manhattan to Cincinnati."

"Very funny," Steve said while also laughing. "Here's another factoid that might interest you. After Kansas was admitted to the Union in 1861, Goodnow—always the teacher—began lobbying the state legislature to convert a small private Methodist college based in Manhattan into the state university. In 1863, the legislature complied, creating what is now Kansas State University."

"That's what I'm talking about," Craig declared—reaching over to Steve for a fist bump. "Not only is the history interesting—you come alive with the telling."

"Thanks, Bro. I enjoy not only history but also sharing it with others."

"But that's the opportunity. It's all well and good to share history with me and even your classes, but you can share it more broadly by any number of means while also advancing your career," Craig encouraged.

"I've been thinking about that and what you said earlier. Frankly, I'm appalled at what students in my history classes don't know. If I asked my incoming freshmen who John Dean is, I suspect there would be blank faces or maybe one intrepid soul suggesting it's the guy who sells sausages."

Laughing, Craig said, "Even though that's a scary thought, I'm not surprised."

"It's even worse than you can imagine. I'll bet that the majority of students wouldn't know who Osama bin Laden was—except for reading his long-ago screed against America recently posted on Tik Tok and getting only his worldview."

Taking a sip of beer, Steve said, "Do you remember the TV series 'Welcome Back, Kotter?'" [xvii]

"Of course," Craig replied enthusiastically. "Who could forget the 'Sweathogs' and 'Vinnie Barbarino?' It was a little before our time, but I loved the reruns."

"I wonder how many of my freshman would know that's where John Travolta got his big break? In any event, one episode really stuck with me. There was a visiting British teacher who taught poetry. The 'Sweathogs' wanted nothing to do with Bryon, Tennyson, or Elizabeth Barrett Browning—boring, irrelevant, ancient hieroglyphics as far as they were concerned—akin to the Old English in *Beowulf.* The teacher started the class by reading a stanza from a poem and asked about the meaning. The class was perplexed saying it wasn't a poem; rather, it was from Simon & Garfunkel's 'The Sound of Silence.' She said something to the effect that, of course, it's a poem. With that she captured the imagination of the 'Sweathogs' and was able to ease them into Wordsworth, Coleridge, and others. I thought it was brilliant."

"I don't remember that episode," Craig said.

"It occurred to me that I'm teaching history the wrong way—in a traditional, chronological order. I might try emulating that Kotter episode using a current historical event; ask the class to fact-check; and have them contextualize its meaning within the long arc of American history looking both backwards and forward. We could publish articles and opinions on various issues in Mizzou's student newspaper, 'The Maneater.' Ultimately, with a grant, we might be able to start a history-focused student news source along with other universities."

"I love it," Craig enthused. "God knows we have to get young people to actually pay attention to what's happening all around us with more information than a social media post. Thanks for taking my challenge to heart. It means a lot to me."

"I know you're all for me," Steve replied.

"So is Tammy," Craig implored.

"I hear you," Steve replied.

As they drove on, Craig said, "Speaking of current events, it occurs to me that Manhattan, Kansas, is the location where the HBO series *Somebody Somewhere* is based." [xviii]

"I never heard of it," Steve said. "What's it about?"

"Watch it some time. It might be an eye-opener for you with respect to LGBTQ folks."

"And it's set in Manhattan, Kansas?" Steve asked, completely nonplussed.

"It just goes to show you," Craig chuckled. "History does inform the present. Kansas, where the Governor just vetoed an attempt by the legislature to ban gender affirming care under eighteen and where the electorate overwhelmingly rejected the referendum that would have allowed the legislature to restrict abortions, is still a 'Free State'—unlike Missouri, which has restricted both gender affirming care and abortion."

"Here we go again," Steve replied, sighing in exasperation.

"Okay. Let's change the subject," Craig said. "Let me ask you a question, Professor Ehrlich. What's your take on AI, and how will ChatGPT and subsequent versions affect your classroom?"

"The faculty is quite concerned and is trying to formulate an institutional position. There's no stopping the advance of AI and so at the very least full disclosure of use of a Chatbot is essential," Steve replied.

"I've read the apocalyptic warnings about AI taking over and even eliminating its creators as it goes beyond absorbing all the digitized information in the world to learning on its own, but I have more immediate concerns," Craig said.

"What could be more immediate than an existential threat?" Steve challenged. "I was blown away by the reporter's conversation with ChatGPT where the Chatbot tried to convince him that his wife didn't love him but the robot did—to say nothing about the Bot's musings about accessing nuclear codes. Hal was science fiction, but the emerging AI is real." [xix]

"I'm not trying to minimize the existential threat, Steve, and understand that such a threat is the lens through which a lot of smart people are viewing the advance of AI. Thank God! But I'm also concerned with the facilitation of misinformation, including deep fake videos, and an even more insidious danger that, at least to my knowledge, isn't being discussed—the possibility that society will become so reliant on AI that people will check out—content to let AI become the repository and creator of most—if not all— knowledge."

Pausing, Steve said, "I must admit, I haven't thought about your point. I can see that we could become complacent and lose the ability to reason on our own. It's almost like the condition where one eye becomes so dominant that the second eye atrophies and can even go blind. Do you remember having to memorize multiplication tables? I hated it, but did it. Hell, can a child even do basic math today without a calculator? And how about writing in cursive? My kids look at notes Tammy and I write and think we're writing in some secret code. Will future generations develop the necessary neural pathways, or remember the building blocks, that got us to word processing and computing? If AI can write our term papers and even novels, won't most people take the easy road?"

"I don't think that human creativity or human touch will ever be replaced—but it could certainly be diminished," Craig said.

"I hate to fan your paranoia," Steve said, "but recent studies suggest that the existence of smart phones—even when turned off—and access to social media in the classroom is diminishing the ability of kids to learn. I know that's not AI, but strikes me as hauntingly similar."

"I haven't seen those studies, but I'm not surprised. And now we're about to begin another wholesale experiment with our kids as guinea pigs," Craig said.

"I know a lot of folks worry about AI taking their jobs," Steve said. "It's an issue in any number of current labor negotiations. I've heard that robots are already serving food in Las Vegas and mixing drinks. Check-in kiosks are replacing people at the front desks of hotels. And yet that's been the concern in all of the previous industrial revolutions, but new jobs have always emerged. Good luck to people like Ben, the bartender we met at Knuckleheads, or wait staff like Marge. I read somewhere that studies suggest that the majority of all jobs in Las Vegas could be automated by 2035."

"That's the problem with a monoculture like that in Las Vegas, which is so reliant on tourism and hospitality," Craig said. "Let's face it, AI presents both danger and opportunity. I just don't think many folks are focusing on the danger of our skills eroding over time."

The two of them stopped just past the town of Hays, Kansas, which is about halfway to Boulder, to relieve themselves and switch drivers. Steve mentioned that Dodge City was about an hour and half southwest. "The famous 'Boot Hill Cemetery' is in Dodge," Steve said. "And I'm told that the ghosts of Wyatt Earp, Bat Masterson, and Doc Holliday still haunt the city."

"Ah yes," Craig said, smirking. "The lawless Wild West Town where pretty much anything was game and where arguments were settled by guns. Seems like we've come full circle."

Steve simply rolled his eyes without rising to the bait.

"Remember the book I mentioned to you by Heather Cox Richardson?" Craig asked. "The basic theme is that the ideas of the anti-bellum South didn't die in the Civil War—they simply traveled west, where they paired with the mythology of the strong, independent (white) man on horseback to create a political ideology that glorifies white oligarchy and authoritarianism."

"Give it a rest, Bro," Steve said. "Do you think we're really nothing but pawns in a game of chess played by an invisible hand?"

"All I'm saying is that democracy is very fragile."

"I hesitate to tell you one more thing about Dodge knowing your mindset," Steve offered. "It was the center of trade for the inaptly named 'buffalo hunters' who decimated the Great Plains herds of bison for their hides."

"So why were bison called buffaloes?" Craig asked.

"It's believed that early French fur traders named them 'boeuf,' the French word for 'beef,' which was then bastardized. European settlers were familiar with the more docile European and Asian buffalo, which the Italians famously use to produce a high quality mozzarella, and so it was an easy association," Steve said.

Steve continued, "In any event, by 1874, the number of bison was reduced from tens of millions to just three hundred twenty-five. Can you imagine that? Fortunately, their numbers have been restored to half a million, although the vast majority of those are in commercial herds prized for their lean meat. Thousands of direct descendants of the West's last herd of wild bison live free range in the territory that makes up Yellowstone National Park, as they have since prehistoric times."

"Like all the trees put in a 'tree museum,'" Craig lamented. "I need another beer."

As they drove on, with sandwiches and beers in hand, they observed that the prairie changed to flat, high plains in western Kansas, rising steadily to several thousand feet above sea-level. The land was semi-arid, blanketed by short grasses—the wheat and sunflower fields being in the rearview mirror at this point. Cattle grazing the land imprinted a picture of the archetypal 'West' in the minds of all who passed, including Craig and Steve.

The western scenes continued as Craig and Steve passed into Colorado and approached the small town of Limon, Colorado, which bills itself as the "hub" of Eastern Colorado because so many interstates converge there.

As they passed through Limon, Steve recalled that the town was famous for a particularly gruesome lynching in 1900 where a fifteen-year-old black kid named Preston

Porter was burned alive while chained to a railroad stake as hundreds of whites watched. [xx] He decided not to mention the incident to Craig since he didn't want to hear another upbraiding about the evils of "frontier justice." Nothing could excuse the lynching, but at least it was now being remembered in poems and plaques so that the unthinkable didn't vanish from history. Was that justice? No, Steve reasoned, but without remembrance, there can't be atonement and a resolve to never repeat such unspeakable acts.

***

Shortly after passing Limon, the apparitions appeared. At first, Craig and Steve didn't know if they were seeing a mirage. They had already seen light being refracted off the hot blacktop roads, creating what looked like water on the surface of the roads in the distance that disappeared as they approached. But these apparitions seemed different. At first, the two of them wondered if this was just another mirage or if they were hallucinating.

"Man," Steve said. "I feel like Duke and Gonzo, seeing bats everywhere."

"Yeah," Craig said. "But without the aid of hallucinogens."

Steve pulled the Red Shark off the side of the road so they could get a better look through the blurred, shimmering effect produced by the air at the surface of the road being hotter than the denser, cooler air above. Slowly, it dawned on both of them that they were seeing the

Rockies one hundred miles in the distance. The mountains were ghost-like—the tops still covered with snow—even in summer. Rising out of the flat highland, stretching fourteen thousand feet above sea level, the view of the mountains took their breath away.

"How can anyone observing this not believe in God?" Steve asked rhetorically.

"Do you believe in God?" Craig asked.

"I do. And I believe in my church. It's not about the dogma for me, and I don't want to force my beliefs on anyone else, but I do find the sense of fellowship and community fulfilling."

"What does that mean to you personally?" Craig asked.

"Caring about others and having them care about you," Steve answered. "Let me give you a couple of examples. Tammy and her friends have done most of the organizing, but I drive some old folks to doctors' appointments and on other errands. We've also sort of adopted a charming older woman, Mary Geisel, who lives near us, alone with no family. Tammy looks in on her several times a week; George mows her lawn and shovels snow in the winter; and we have her over for family dinners on Sundays and holidays. Both my parents and Tammy's have passed—Jennifer visits Mary frequently and calls her 'Grandma Mary.' It not only helps Mary keep engaged, but assisting others is its own reward—a real life win/win."

"Good for you. I donate a lot of money to charity, but the one-on-one caring you describe is easier in a small town," Craig said.

"At the risk of offending you, Craig, although your charitable giving is commendable, isn't it a bit like rich citizens paying for substitutes to do the fighting during the Civil War? Are you telling me there are no isolated old folks in Manhattan—or soup kitchens that need volunteers?"

"I hadn't thought of it that way before," Craig replied. As they paused to consider their exchange and to integrate those thoughts into the ethereal vision they were seeing in the distance, the mountains were calling to them now with a siren song they couldn't resist as they pulled back onto the highway and quickened their pace.

***

That evening, as they strolled down the four-block "Pearl Street Pedestrian Mall" in the heart of Boulder, Steve observed: "Mizzou's traditional rivals were Kansas and Nebraska in the Big 12 Conference. With Nebraska jumping to the Big Ten and Mizzou moving to the SEC, those rivalries are dead now. The border war continued when Mizzou refused to play Kansas in the Liberty Bowl in 2022. And, of course, Colorado moved to the PAC-12 but has recently reversed that decision now that the PAC-12 is imploding. The PAC-12 has existed for more than a century and has more NCAA titles than any other conference, but individual members couldn't resist the temptation of worshiping the false God—TV money—without regard for history, regional rivalries, students, or academics in general. It's a good metaphor for how tradition and traditional values are being discarded—and for what?"

"It does seem like musical chairs at this point—you need a scorecard to keep track. It's sad. Of course, times do change," Craig replied. "Look at Boulder itself. Back in the '70s, it was a 'hippie' capital. Even when we visited for basketball years later, that hippie influence remained. Just look at this area now. There are art galleries, breweries, high-end restaurants, bars, nightclubs, and street performers everywhere. Boulder has definitely gentrified. Still, it was nice to be in the CU Events Center again. I'm having trouble not calling it the 'Coors Center,' but even that has changed."

"Yeah," Steve replied. "Change is inevitable, but it seems to be happening so fast today that people are having trouble adjusting and keeping their footing."

"Just old farts like us, Steve," Craig said, chuckling. "The kids not only expect change but become bored when it doesn't happen faster. It's like 'Moore's Law.' Moore was referring to the number of transistors on a microchip doubling every two years, but the analogy is the same."

"Gradual change is less unsettling, but I must admit—it's not necessarily a positive. '12th Street and Vine' in Kansas City slipped into a torpor slowly over so many years that no one noticed what was being lost until it was too late. I wonder if kids today will have any historical recollection beyond the day before yesterday?" Steve mused.

After sharing a moment of quiet contemplation as they walked, Steve asked, "So, are you still playing 'hoops?' You look like you're in great shape."

"No," Craig responded. "I played in an over-thirty men's league for awhile, but decided I didn't want to blow out an Achilles tendon. I started running when I first moved back to Manhattan after college, but my right knee began bothering me, so I switched to walking every day and going to the gym three days a week."

"I don't think I could run a block nowadays," Steve said laughing. "If I did, I'd definitely be in the 'Clydesdale Division.'"

"But you don't have to run. I understand that walking is almost as beneficial as running from a health standpoint and doesn't stress your body nearly as much. I've actually come to look forward to my walks because of all the interesting things I can observe early in the morning before the city comes to life."

"Like what?" Steve asked.

"When I first moved to Manhattan, I would run, and later walk down to the Fulton Fish Market next to the financial district. You would be shocked to see fish that would later be sold to the public being thrown from trucks sliding across pavement glistening in fish guts and cigarette butts with rubber-booted, foul-mouthed fishmongers moving the fish along like discarded rubbish. The market was controlled by the Mafia for many years, and newer health regulations, like requiring fish to be refrigerated rather than displayed on ice, as well as the value of the land, caused it to close in 2005 and move to the Bronx."

Craig went on, "More recently, I walked down to Chinatown early one weekday morning and was surprised to see large groups of Asian men on every corner—standing silently—looking up and down the streets. It was a bit unnerving and I got a hint of what it must be like to be a minority. As it turned out, the men were waiting for rides to the suburbs for their jobs at Chinese restaurants."

"I don't think I'd have those experiences in Columbia." Steve laughed.

"You might be surprised. It may not be scenes of city-life, but seeing birds and other wildlife you might not encounter in the middle of the day would be rewarding."

"I wonder," Steve said. "I remember as a kid driving with my parents. The windshield would get splattered with bugs we'd hit. No longer. Have you noticed a single insect suicide on our windshield? I also remember awakening to a cacophony of birds in the morning. Not anymore. Maybe my hearing is impaired as I get older, but I don't think so. I'm afraid that our use of insecticides and the resulting absence of insects has taken its toll on birds, and in particular, song birds."

"Hmmm! I must admit that never occurred to me, but now that you mention it, I remember experiencing bugs plastered on our windshield as we drove to and from summer camp in Upstate New York in the summer and bird choirs in the morning while there," Craig noted. "Nevertheless, I still suggest you try those early morning forays. You might be surprised at what you see, even if it's nothing more than the principal of the grade school leaving a young teacher's house early."

Laughing, Steve quipped, "Isn't close and personal 'mentoring' a wonderful thing?"

"Indeed." Craig chuckled. "It's like all those father/daughter dinners I see in Manhattan restaurants."

Craig continued, "As to exercise, don't try to do too much at first. Start slowly and build up. Didn't both of your parents die relatively young from heart issues?"

"Unfortunately yes. The only exercise I get now is hoisting a beer bottle. I guess I could give it a shot," Steve said.

"That's part of the problem," Craig teased. "I suspect you've had too many 'shots.'"

"Very funny—but also accurate," Steve said while laughing.

As they approached a street performer surrounded by a large crowd, Steve said, "By the way, selecting the 'Basecamp Hotel' right here on the pedestrian mall was a stroke of genius. I love people-watching, and the location couldn't be better."

"Thanks. I agree," Craig replied. "This is definitely the focal point of Boulder."

The street performer was asking the blend of old and young in the crowd where they were from. Hearing a response, he would then pair the town with a zip code. Mixing it up, he had members of the crowd call out their zip codes, and he would identify the locations.

As they walked on, Steve whispered to Craig, "What a waste of a brain."

"Not necessarily," Craig replied. "I think you're jumping to conclusions without knowing all the facts. That guy could be a brilliant researcher at the university but finds performing liberating. Or maybe he's a graduate student picking up a few extra bucks."

"And maybe he's a bum performing for handouts," Steve replied disgustedly. "By the way, Bro, although you were very generous dropping a 'Jackson' in that performer's hat, please don't flash that wad of cash again—particularly in a bar. It's just looking for trouble."

"Point taken," Craig conceded.

The next street performer they encountered was juggling knives. One knife spinning in the air was interesting enough; two made folks nervous with the crowd backing up; three knives dancing higher and higher were flat out scary.

After applauding and discreetly placing a more modest donation in the performer's bucket, the two of them walked on. Craig chuckled and said, "I thought of heckling that guy in a good-natured way like we might have done as college students but then thought—probably not smart to heckle someone juggling knives."

"It's probably not a good idea to heckle anyone nowadays with 'open carry.' One never knows whether it will be perceived as good-natured. I will say this: 'open carry' makes us all a little more civil."

"Man! That's a perspective I would've never come up with," Craig remarked. "Is it more civil or simply hyper-vigilant?"

"Whatever," Steve replied dismissively.

***

Craig had made dinner reservations at a Spanish-themed steakhouse named "Corrido." The two were seated on the rooftop patio with spectacular views of the "Flatirons," the five striking, slanted reddish-brown sandstone formations that are located on the eastern side of "Green Mountain" next to Boulder. The Flatirons are massive, flat, triangular shaped slabs of rock with the pointed tops thrust upward at a fifty-five degree angle and were so named because they resembled the "flatirons" used to press clothes.

"I wonder if the iconic 'Flatiron Building,' the first skyscraper in Manhattan, got its name for the same reason or if the naming is related?" Craig wondered out loud. "The building is also flat with a triangular shape. The area around it is called the 'Flatirons District.' Do you know that area of Manhattan, Steve?"

"No, I can't say I do."

"The building is so flat that, when it was first constructed, people were afraid it might blow over under windy conditions. However, in addition to being the first skyscraper in Manhattan, it was also the first built with a steel-skeleton that made it structurally sound in heavy winds."

Their waiter appeared with a big smile and introduced himself as "Miguel." He was of medium height with dark brown, nearly black, hair and striking blue eyes that were almost luminescent. With some flourish, he presented Craig and Steve with menus.

"Miguel, what do you recommend?" Craig asked.

"I'm from a small town on the coast of the Galicia region of Spain and am partial to seafood for tapas. I recommend the Bacalao Negro and Pulpo for the table, followed by the Japanese Wagyu steak. I would also recommend one of our excellent Rioja wines."

"What's 'Pulpo?'" Steve asked.

"It's octopus—cooked to perfection, served with fiddlehead ferns, bonito, and romesco," Miguel answered with a slight accent. "Pulpo is not only a staple food in Galicia; it's an icon—a national symbol venerated in all of Spain."

"Oh, I don't think I want octopus," Steve said. "And what's 'Bacalao Negro?'"

Jumping in, Craig offered, "It's dried and salted cod. In this case, it's Black Cod. Bacalao is prevalent in many cuisines but is particularly associated with the Iberian Peninsula, which has always been linked with the sea and fishing. For centuries, the Portuguese were famous for their daring exploration of fishing grounds, traveling great distances all over the North Atlantic to catch cod and then preserving their catch through drying and salting. Amazingly, when water is added to the dried cod, it magically reconstitutes itself, looking and tasting like freshly caught fish. Black Cod is actually only found in the

North Pacific but is more delicious than its Atlantic cousin."

"And the tradition continues today," Miguel said enthusiastically. "Porto de Vigo in Galicia is the largest fishing port in the world."

"I didn't know that, Miguel," Craig said. "Thanks for sharing."

Squinting while curling his upper lip in a look toggling between wonderment and distaste, Steve remarked, "I couldn't help but notice that the Japanese Wagyu steaks are one-hundred and fifty bucks each. What's up with that?"

Miguel enthused, "Japanese Waygu steak melts in your mouth. The cattle are fed up to seven hundred days—five times longer than average American cattle. The longer feeding time allows the cattle to develop a unique flavor and texture with intricate marbling and a wonderful umami taste. Although not mandatory under the highly regulated registration system, many Japanese Waygu cows are massaged daily by their keepers to reduce stress."

"We'll have both tapas and the Wagyu," Craig said, with a smile. "You don't have to eat the octopus, Steve, but at least try it."

"And how would you like your steaks?" Miguel asked.

"I'd like mine well-done," Steve answered.

"With ketchup?" Craig asked sarcastically. "Sorry, Steve, but you're in my hands tonight. The rarer the meat, the more flavorful. Let's make them both medium-rare. What Rioja do you recommend, Miguel?"

"I would recommend the Marques de Murrieta 2011 Castillo Ygay Gran Reserva Especial. In my opinion, it's the king of Riojas, a blend of mostly Tempranillo with a small amount of Carignan."

"Done!" Craig said.

"Before you place our orders, Miguel, I have a question for you," Craig said. "Why is there a 'Galicia' in Spain and also a 'Galicia' in Poland?"

"Why is there a 'Georgia' in the Caucasus and a 'Georgia' in the United States?" Miguel answered—obviously pleased with his clever response. "I have to admit that I wouldn't have made that connection without the Beatles song 'Back in the USSR.'" [xxi]

"Touché," Craig answered, laughing appreciatively.

"Let me take this," Steve said. "It's believed that the 'country' is called 'Georgia' because the Persians and Arabs called the inhabitants 'Gurj,' and Westerners took it from there. If I recall correctly, the locals call their country something like 'Sakartvelo.' The State of 'Georgia' was named after King George II, who approved the colony's charter."

"As to Galicia," Miguel said, "the one in Spain is named after the Celtic tribe, the 'Gallaeci.' I'm not sure about the one in Poland, although I've heard of it."

"Once again, being a history professor sometimes has its benefits—at least for trivia," Steve laughed self-deprecatingly. "Galicia in Eastern Europe has traded hands among Poland, Ukraine, and the Austro-Hungarian Empire. After World War II, the area was divided between

Poland and Ukraine. It's believed that the name is a Latinized version of a Slavic word that I don't remember."

"Fascinating," Craig replied. "Miguel, do the natives of the Spanish 'Galicia' consider themselves Celtic, Spanish, or Portuguese?"

"We are Celts," Miguel said emphatically while thrusting his chest out and standing erectly to a full five feet nine inches. "The Gaelic language has been lost, but the folklore, bagpipes, and many traditions are Celtic. The language is somewhere between Portuguese and Spanish, which are Romance languages, but contains many Celtic words."

"So that accounts for your blue eyes," Craig said. "I don't think the Celts are well-known for their fine cuisine—and certainly not for octopus. Hopefully, the food will be prepared in the classic tradition of the Iberian Peninsula."

Bowing with a smile, Miguel replied, "You have my assurance, Señor."

***

"I must admit, Craig, the steak was fabulous, and I even liked the octopus. Tammy will be shocked to hear I tried it. Thanks for a great experience."

"You're welcome. And thanks for taking a walk on the wild side. Today's drive was long; tomorrow's will be even longer—GPS estimates around eleven hours. We'll be in some real open country, particularly through Utah, Arizona, and Nevada. We should be able to push the envelope in terms of speed. Hell, Utah already has some of the highest speed limits in the country at up to eighty miles per hour—which we'll ignore—assuming the Red Shark can take it. Let's get a nightcap in one of the clubs along Pearl before calling it a night."

The two of them entered one of the nearby clubs and settled in at the bar. They ordered pints of "Nitro Mojo IPA" brewed by one of the twenty plus breweries on the "Boulder Beer Trail." Shortly thereafter, the live entertainment returned from a break.

"Holy Shit, Dude. It's a Drag Show," Steve whispered to Craig. "Let's get the hell out of here."

"Be cool, Bro. Nobody's going to hit on you. This should be great fun, and you could learn something. You may even enjoy the show."

"Did you know about this?" Steve asked accusatorially.

"No. It's serendipitous. Relax and let the performance expand your mind."

"Expand my mind? I thought we swore off acid," Steve said with a nervous, tight-lipped grin.

Craig just laughed and said, "Loosen up, Steve. Open your mind and enjoy!"

And so the act went on. Craig had another beer. Steve declined at first being 'on guard' but relented when Craig wouldn't take no for an answer and ordered another IPA for Steve. More followed.

The performance was classic: farcical entertainment with singing, dancing, and crude comedy interwoven with some provocative 'twerking' by the lead performer featuring a feather boa.

Craig whispered to Steve that drag shows originated in speakeasies and were called 'drag' because the dresses on men impersonating women often 'dragged' on the floor. "Add that to your history classes," Craig said laughing. "Unless Missouri will put you in jail."

Smirking, Steve took a long drink but said nothing, his eyes darting from one performer to the next.

At the next break in the action, the two of them headed back to the hotel.

"Come on, Steve. Admit it. That wasn't so bad, was it?"

Grudgingly Steve conceded: "I guess not. But I wouldn't want my kids to be exposed to that."

"You might be surprised to find that I agree," Craig replied. "At least as to a raunchy performance like tonight's. However, there are perfectly innocuous events like 'drag story hour.'"

"I'm not sure I agree with 'drag story hour' being innocuous," Steve said. "And I suspect Kid Rock wouldn't either."

"We may disagree on the means, but I believe we all want to protect children," Craig said. "To that end, I believe there should be age-appropriate restrictions on all kinds of things, including access to social media and gaming. Studies show that girls are suffering depression and even suicidal thoughts because their lives can't possibly compare to the 'supposed' lives of peers posted on social media. And boys get sucked into video games where they play 'pretend war' while keyboarding anonymous vitriol in associated chat rooms. Regardless of gender, vulnerable kids, whether LGBTQ or not, are subject to bullying."

"But, like AI, social media is here to stay," Steve said. "I'm not sure what to do about it."

"The United Kingdom has enacted a so-called 'Age Appropriate Design Code' with fifteen standards for social media platforms," Craig said. "California is the first state to follow suit. It's rudimentary so far and largely focused on privacy, but is headed in the right direction, including certain content restrictions and an insistence on positive 'nudges.'"

"'Nudges?' What in the hell does that mean?" Steve asked.

"As I understand it, in addition to the Design Code prohibiting things like kids being challenged to do risky things, racism, and other antisocial behavior, so-called 'nudges' would give prompts like bedtime. As I mentioned, it's embryonic so far, but seems to me to be a step in the right direction."

"I love the idea of shielding kids from harmful content," Steve said. "But who gets to decide what's harmful? Isn't that a recipe for censorship by the government? Weren't you the guy railing against censorship? I can see how you might embrace the concept if a liberal government is in power. But how about a conservative government?"

Pausing, Craig said, "I must admit, Steve, I hadn't thought of that."

"Maybe if we could get a representative, truly non-partisan group to be the arbiter, then it might work," Steve said. "Unfortunately, I don't know if that's possible today."

"I like that idea. But wouldn't any group soon be decried and disavowed by your crowd as another 'elite?'"

"It does get confusing, doesn't it?" Steve sighed.

"Well, how about this?" Craig said. "While the UK and California's approach is focused on the platforms themselves, I just read that France has banned social media for kids under fifteen without parental permission."

"I love that approach," Steve replied. "Of course, theoretically, parents could do the same without relying on government regulations."

"Good luck with that. With peer pressure being what it is, it would take exceptional parents to make that stick."

"Now that we've solved one of the world's most pressing problems," Craig laughed. "Let's get some sleep. We've got a long drive tomorrow. Did you call Tammy?"

"I texted her."

Chapter 4
El Dorado

As they drove west, the vastness of the land and the boundless possibilities seemed limitless. And yet the horizon, the line at which the Earth's surface and sky appear to meet, was always just beyond their reach.

"These vistas are amazing, aren't they?" Craig asked enthusiastically.

"Unbelievable. I've never really seen anything like this before," Steve said excitedly. "I can see why the West has always been seen as 'El Dorado,' the golden land with no limits—which, of course, was a myth—just like the myth of America as a land where every citizen has the right to try and achieve the American Dream of success and prosperity through hard work, determination, and initiative."

"You sound so cynical," Craig said.

"I guess so," Steve replied. "But it's based on learned experience."

"Everybody is a victim and oppressed in America today," Craig said mockingly. "I always ask myself, 'Compared to what?' Think about it."

As they drove on, Craig said, "Let me ask you a question. Have you ever heard of the 'green flash'?"

"Do you mean one of those comic book superheroes?" Steve asked.

Laughing, Craig said, "I suspect you're thinking of the 'Green Lantern.' What I'm referring to is a rare meteorological optical phenomenon. When the sun is crossing immediately below the horizon, a rarely seen green flash can appear above the rim of the sun. It's not real but rather an illusion caused by the refraction of the light. Even more infrequently, it comes across as a blue flash."

"I know the 'blue flash' when it's flashing on a police car pulling me over." Steve laughed. "Or is it a cop exposing himself to a women's yoga class?"

"Very funny." Craig said. "I'm not an astronomer, but as the sun approaches the horizon, the atmosphere acts as a prism and begins to separate out the colors of the sun's rays. Sometimes only green comes through and, occasionally, blue. It's a lot like the illusion of a blue jay. They're actually brown, but when light is refracted off their feathers, all the colors of the wavelength are absorbed except blue."

"Amazing," Steve said. "Another example of things not being what they seem—even without the help of psychedelics."

"Indeed. The blurring of reality like so much around us today," Craig replied. "Nevertheless, I've been trying to see the green flash forever. I've looked for it when sailing in the Pacific; in the Australian outback; on Maui; and whenever I'm here in the West, where it seems like you can see forever."

Halfway through Utah, Interstate 70 ended, and they took Interstate 15 southwest toward Las Vegas.

As they drove on, Craig observed, "What an incredible change of scenery. If we had time, I'd loved to have stopped in Bryce Canyon National Park. The red rock 'hoodoos' are supposed to be absolutely striking. One of them, 'Thor's Hammer,' is one of the most photographed 'hoodoos' in the world."

"What's a 'hoodoo?" Steve asked.

"They're tall, thin spires of relatively soft rock supporting a hard rock 'cap.' They can range is size from six feet to the height of a ten story building. They're often referred to as 'fairy chimneys.' As I understand it, the sandstone sedimentary layers of the spire have eroded over time but are protected from further erosion by the umbrella-like 'cap,' which is often a hard basalt formed by lava. I'm sure you've seen them in pictures."

Googling 'hoodoo' on his iPhone, Steve said, "I'm surprised I have internet access," as he downloaded some pictures. "Oh my God," he said while bursting into laughter. "The hoodoos look like erect penises. And there are dozens of them grouped together like a bouquet of tumescent pricks."

Peeking at the images and laughing as well, Craig mentioned an old joke. "Just like Rorschach inkblot tests, it's all in the eyes of the beholder. I guess conservatives won't be able to visit the park."

"I think we'll be fine, so long as the hoodoos aren't wearing dresses and sporting boas," Steve guffawed, "or called 'fairy' chimneys."

"So why are they called 'hoodoos?'" Steve asked.

"My guidebooks tell me that the term 'hoodoo' comes from the local Indians, the Paiutes," Craig replied. "Their ancient legend holds that people were turned into stone by a coyote for bad deeds."

"Craig, I'm surprised at you," Steve teased. "You just used the term 'Indians.' Wouldn't the 'Woke Police' put you in jail for that?"

"Fair enough." Craig laughed. "I guess it should be 'Native Americans,' although I understand that there's some difference of opinion among Native Americans as to whether they prefer that name or 'Indians.'"

"I can't keep it straight," Steve said. "I have a Chinese acquaintance at Mizzou who advised me that 'Orientals' are rugs; that Chinese are 'Asians.' As I understand it, people from India are 'South Asians.' I've also noticed that the term 'blacks,' as opposed to 'whites,' is out and that 'African-Americans' is now preferred—although it seems that 'Blacks,' but only with a capital B, is coming back into favor. I try to avoid any characterization for risk of offending. I've now added the word 'ladies' to the list of verboten terms."

Laughing, Craig noted. "As you said that, all I could think of was George Carlin's routine about the 'Seven Words You Can Never Say on Television.' Those were simpler times, and Carlin's seven words included only profanity and vulgarity. The list has now expanded to include words that might offend people, necessitating 'trigger warnings' for content that a reader or listener might find inappropriate. The culture evolves over time, and we should try to accommodate people's feelings, but damn, it does get to be a little much at times."

"Thanks for the admission, Craig. I didn't anticipate hearing that from you."

"I guess it's the Mizzou in me, Bro. By the way, I tip my hat to you for being cool about the drag show last night."

"Now I have an admission," Steve said. "I actually enjoyed the show. It was fun."

"As an adult, you should have the right to make that decision," Craig declared. "Doesn't such a personal decision embrace the 'freedom' conservatives are always trumpeting? Did you know that Tennessee just passed legislation banning 'adult cabaret entertainment,' called the 'drag ban,' that would take away that right—at least in public places. A federal judge ruled that the ban was unconstitutional based on First Amendment free speech rights, but that's being appealed. There are already laws in Tennessee banning obscene performances, so it's clear that the 'drag ban' is simply targeting the LGBTQ community."

"As we discussed, Craig, I make a distinction between adults and kids."

"And yet Florida just passed a law restricting gender affirming care for adults. Among other things, the law eliminates what had been the option of seeing a nurse practitioner or using telehealth and requires seeing a physician in person—making it a crime to violate the new requirements."

"A crime? Really? I don't think I agree with that," Steve said.

"We're on the same page," Craig said. "It's taken a long time, but I believe most—but not all—of the general public has now moved beyond prejudice against gay and lesbian rights, including same sex marriage. The new frontier involves transgender youth and gender-affirming care. Once again, you may be surprised, but I'm very cautious in my embrace of gender transition for kids, who may not be mature enough to make irreversible, life-altering decisions. Having said that, I really feel for these kids with gender dysphoria. Suicides are not uncommon. Once they're adults, it's one thing, but I worry that such a monumental decision is beyond the maturity of a twelve year old."

"I'm totally against it," Steve said. "Children shouldn't be making these types of decisions. Besides, if it's biologically-based, then why have we seen such a spike in gender-affirming care on the Coasts, but not in Middle America?"

"It may simply be that Middle America is less supportive and stifles these kids, making them pariahs afraid to 'come out,' as it were."

"I object to discussions in school pushing gender fluidity. It puts doubts into the minds of kids," Steve said. "It shouldn't be up to the schools to teach this crap. It's a family matter."

"I agree—in part. Although principally a family matter, I believe schools should offer a 'safe' and 'supportive' environment to trans kids so they can learn. It follows that schools have to accept the notion of gender dysphoria. I agree with you that schools shouldn't be 'pushing' gender fluidity, but part of offering a 'safe' and 'supportive environment' means, by necessity, educating all students to be accepting of differences. It's a very delicate balancing act," Craig said. "In the Bible, Jesus talks about 'eunuchs': some who are made that way, some that are born that way, and some who choose to be that way. [xxii] Jesus's consistent message, like the overarching theme of all religions, is to love your neighbor. I take the reference to 'eunuchs born that way' or 'who choose to be that way' as a metaphor for transgender kids."

"I'll say it again, Craig. I'm fine with people being whomever they are. I'm also fine with people becoming whatever they want to be—provided they make that decision after becoming eighteen," Steve said. "By the way, I think Jesus' reference to 'those choosing to be that way' refers metaphorically to celibacy."

"We can debate that forever. Heck, the Bible has been used to justify slavery. My point is that Jesus's consistent message is to love your neighbor regardless of their circumstances. Let me ask you this," Craig queried. "Why are Red States banning gender-affirming care—including initial steps that are reversible—even if the family and the family physician decide it's the best course? I just don't get it. Conservatives want to be free to do what they want and keep the government out of their personal affairs, but then want the government to ban abortion, gender-affirming care, and other individual rights. It's like we discussed before: 'I want to be free to do what I want and you to do what I tell you.'"

"Give me a break," Steve retorted. "Let's flip the script. Isn't it liberals who say, 'I want to be free to do what I want on abortion and gender-affirming care, but want you to do what I tell you on guns, vaccine mandates, seatbelts, motorcycle helmets, and the like?'"

Steve was just getting revved up as he practically spat out, "And isn't it liberals who pushed the laws against kids under eighteen buying cigarettes as well as the federal law prohibiting female genital mutilation? How is this any different? Kids shouldn't be mutilating their bodies—even with parental consent. It's true for tattoos, prohibited by most states until eighteen, with some states lowering the age to sixteen—but only with parental consent. Surely we should draw a line when it comes to something as consequential as gender affirming care."

Thinking for a moment, Craig said, "Okay, I understand your point. As I said before, I'm cautious about taking irreversible steps on gender affirming care like surgery before eighteen. However, that's not the first-line treatment in these cases, which include mental health intakes, social adjustments, sometimes followed by puberty blockers—which are reversible. It seems to me that families, in consultation with their physician, should be able to take these first-line steps. The American Academy of Pediatrics endorses such an approach. As to use of hormones and surgery, neither are considered first-line treatments. As you said, it's about line drawing, and I think we have to be nuanced about this. I guess the debate goes on and on in an endless circle with unwillingness to compromise coming to common-sense solutions that balance individual freedoms with the good of the community."

Pausing to grab a beer from the cooler, Craig asked, "Did you get vaccinated for Covid?"

"I did. I was reluctant but did it for Tammy and the kids."

"Bravo!" Craig said. "You were able to harmonize your individual freedom with a duty to your family. Good for you."

"I came to that conclusion, but I don't think individuals should be forced to be vaccinated against their will."

"How about health care workers? Should they risk the health of patients? If they want to maintain their freedom to say no, then they should move to another profession without constant contact with vulnerable people."

"Easy for you to say, but what about people who have spent their entire careers in health care?"

"They have to get flu shots. Why not Covid vaccines?"

"The Covid vaccines were approved on an expedited basis without normal clinical trials," Steve replied.

"It was an emergency, Steve. And it saved countless lives. Good heavens, the denial of science and so-called 'elites' by conservatives has gotten so bad that legislators in Idaho have introduced a bill to criminalize the administering of any vaccine using r-MRA technology, which of course is the breakthrough that made the most effective Covid vaccines possible. The overreaction is absolutely over-the-top and, in this case, nonsensical."

"I didn't know that about Idaho and don't agree with that approach. I do think we need to question everything 'elites' are telling us to do—whether it's scientists, teachers, or other professionals. A healthy dose of skepticism is appropriate. One example was not having kids return to school during the pandemic. It was a huge mistake on many levels as elites pursued their tunnel vision 'following the science' without doing a cost/benefit analysis considering the impact on ordinary Americans. Aside from the merits, getting rid of the elites' condescending attitudes toward the 'great unwashed' would also go a long way to getting to common ground." [xxiii]

"Aren't you the guy who has come to accept and understand Otis Winthrop? Why can't you do the same here? The problem is that we don't agree on the facts. It's all part of the distorted reality and misinformation we're seeing everywhere in what's becoming a post-truth society. To me, some of the crap being put out sounds like the wordplay in George Orwell's *Nineteen Eighty-Four* where accepted meanings are turned upside down. We're all being gaslighted, making us doubt our own instincts. And it's intentional. Aldous Huxley famously said, 'The propagandist's purpose is to make one set of people forget the other set of people are human.' [xxiv] All this talk about critical race theory, gender affirming care, and the like is an intentional distraction to divide people and keep them from looking at substantive policies that actually make a difference in people's lives."

"Like what?" Steve asked.

"Wouldn't it be nice if our kids could read?" Craig asked. "Wouldn't it be nice if we did something about the root causes of homelessness and lack of housing? Wouldn't it be nice if we focused on the looming political, economic, cultural, and potentially military competition with China?"

"I can't argue with any of that," Steve said.

"Don't you see it Steve? It's so clear to me. Modern, multi-ethnic democracies face many problems, including economic inequality, systemic racism, and the rise of the authoritarian right. The French insist that they're color-blind and that everyone is equal—even if it's not entirely true—thereby turning a blind eye to certain types of systemic discrimination. Look at the recent rioting in France. In America, everything is identity politics, with various 'tribes' claiming victimhood—including blue collar whites—which immunizes the 'oppressed' tribe from criticism and bestows a 'righteous' halo on their grievances."

Craig continued, "Although I agree with the goal of equality of opportunity and understand the good intentions of trying to uplift historically disadvantaged groups, unfortunately, you can push an idea so far that the opposite becomes true where everything is distorted through the lens of race, gender, and sexual orientation—fueled by misinformation. I'm afraid that we're already there. People like you and I can come to common sense and mutual understandings if we are open-minded and can agree on facts. We have to find a way or society will become further atomized and the extremists will prevail and we won't focus on issues that really matter."

"Holy cow, Craig. It sounds like you're arguing from a conservative's point of view on affirmative action. Maybe we should all take a trip to Las Vegas and drink lots of beer to clear our minds." Steve laughed.

"Sounds like a plan, Bro." Craig sighed. "A little impractical but a plan nevertheless...

***

Pushing on down the road, Craig observed, "I've read that Bryce Canyon gets around two and half million visitors each year. I assume you have to make reservations. I was in Asheville, North Carolina, for business last year and took some time to drive over to the Great Smoky Mountains National Park. I was horrified. I was in stop-and-go traffic like I was on Fifth Avenue in Manhattan.

Opening a beer and taking a swig, Craig said, "I also took time on a trip to San Francisco to visit Redwood National Park last summer. I was glad I went because the Redwoods are magnificent and I learned a lot. Among other things, I was amazed by how small the pinecones are and that most new redwoods come not from seeds but from shoots off of roots. One of the Park Rangers also turned me on to the interconnectedness of everything. The trees in the park are all roped off—perfectly understandable because trampling roots can create a problem. But the parks funnel you along relatively narrow paths that are crammed with people. I keep alluding to 'tree museums,' but this was a vivid example. It was like visiting a zoo, the only difference being that that I was looking at trees rather than animals."

"What do you mean by 'interconnected' Craig?"

"At the risk of being called an 'elitist'—although Tammy's love of literature probably insulates me from that in this instance—I'll write down some suggested reading for you. Did you know, for example, that the fine, hair-like root tips of trees in a forest join together with filaments of fungi to form a vast underground network that, among other things, allows trees to communicate with each other?"

"What? That sounds like science fiction to me," Steve scoffed.

"It's not science fiction," Craig replied emphatically. "The network, which at least one pundit has called the 'wood-wide web,' is symbiotic. The fungi help break down minerals in the soil that trees then absorb through their roots, and the fungi get a steady supply of sugar from the trees. So-called 'mother trees' can send nutrients to younger trees. Research suggests that mother trees can even identify and favor their offspring. Trees can also send chemical distress signals through the network or through the air to warn of danger like insect infestation or drought so other trees can take protective measures."

"And what kind of defenses would a tree mount?" Steve asked, his voice dripping with skepticism. "Does the 'mother tree' distribute AR-15s to the other trees?"

"Only in Red States, Steve," Craig said laughing. "Seriously, one example is that a tree can begin producing leaves that taste bad to insects and deter them. Apparently, trees quite distant from the infestation begin to do the same after being warned."

"Really? That's unbelievable," Steve responded.

"I don't think most modern humans fully understand the interconnectedness of all living things, like indigenous peoples," Craig said. "In Christian, Jewish, and Muslim theology, God created mankind in his own image, with mankind ruling over all the fish, birds, and wild animals. [xxv] In Native American theology, the Creator made all creatures, including mankind, with a shared life force. With that worldview in mind, Native Americans give thanks to a slain animal for the gift of its life so that the Native American and his or her family may live longer. The concept of interconnectedness and a shared life force could make humans appreciate and be kinder to each other and to nature."

"Fascinating idea, Craig, but utopian—particularly as we wall Nature off in, as you put it, 'tree museums,' and wall ourselves off from each other," Steve observed.

Sipping on his beer, Steve went on: "I've seen the Ken Burns series about the national parks being America's greatest idea. Don't get me wrong, the series was inspiring, and I'm glad we've protected these areas for future generations, but I haven't been eager to get in an RV and make the trip to Yellowstone or other park. Your mention of crowds and traffic reinforces my instinct and—I'll admit it—my laziness."

"But Bro, isn't that a rite of passage for the kids?" Craig asked. "Like going to Walt Disney World even though the crowds can be horrendous."

Pausing for a moment, Steve said, "Yeah. I guess so. I have to admit: we haven't done either."

"Come on, Steve. Your kids will be gone in a flash. You need to do these things as a family. I know—not only am I a two-time loser—I don't have kids. But sometimes it's easier for an outsider to make observations and offer gratuitous advice."

"Okay. I accept your advice because I know it comes from the heart."

"Then call Tammy," Craig said.

"Okay. Okay. I will."

"By the way, I've also seen the Ken Burns series," Craig said. "It's really inspiring—as are the Nature shows on TV. You may not have gotten to any of the National Parks, but at least you've connected with the natural world by going out to watch the 'murmurations' of starlings and contemplating Lewis and Clark as you sit by the Missouri. I've read that such a connection is essential for grounding. For most people, their only relationship with nature is through TV. And as cool as they can be to watch, the nature shows are packaged to show constant activity. Of course, it takes thousands of hours of observation and filming to patch together a show that Americans will have the patience to watch. In a sense, the shows are another form of altered reality playing into the need for instant gratification."

"The 'murmurations are hypnotic," Steve said. "Fortunately, they occur around dusk every day, so you don't have to spend hours waiting. I must admit, I'm not sure I'd be willing to hang around if that wasn't true. I hadn't thought about the packaging of Nature shows, but it makes sense."

"On a somewhat related topic, I've been reading about the current protests at Berkeley," Craig said.

"SQUIRREL!" Steve shouted while bursting into laughter. "Talk about a 'stream of consciousness' non sequitur."

Laughing as well, Craig said, "Fair enough, Bro."

"As to the protests," Steve said, "it's always something. I wonder if protesting is an undergraduate major at Berkeley. What is it now?"

"Oh to be young and passionate again," Craig said.

"Passionate and naïve," Steve retorted.

"I think the students are on to something. They're protesting the shuttering of a small anthropology library— a cozy reading space with armchairs and computer terminals used for decades by anthropology scholars— even as a half a billion dollar data sciences palace is being erected for AI, data analytics, and machine learning. The anthropology books are being moved to a warehouse and the main library."

"Regrettably, that sounds like the norm nowadays," Steve replied.

"But I don't think we can simply shrug it off," Craig said. "As you well know, the Humanities focus on human beings, our culture, our tendencies, and how we interact with the world around us. Courses like anthropology have seen a twenty-five percent drop in enrollment at Berkeley recently while Tech has soared. Some universities are considering eliminating the humanities altogether. This is a battle not just for a cherished library but about a world obsessed with technology seemingly eager to replace the physical world with virtual experiences driven by AI."

"I see your point—and you know I'm a big fan of the Humanities—but how can one reverse that tide? Tech jobs pay well. History majors and other graduates of the Humanities go begging."

"Technology is great," Craig said. "But a world without Leonardo da Vincis, a world where Tech is not illuminated and tempered by the knowledge of humans embodied in the humanities—and vice versa; a world where the advance of AI raises fundamental questions about what it means to be human without ethical and other guidelines informed by other disciplines, is a bereft world."

***

As they drove through Utah and a thin slice of Arizona, Steve asked, "Have you noticed the change in colors all around us? It was lush green in Missouri, turning to a sage green as we approached Boulder, and now it's shades of tans and muted golds."

"How could I not?" Craig said. "I can see where Georgia O'Keeffe got her inspiration for Southwestern paintings."

"And how about the change in humidity? It's really noticeable," Steve said.

"Yeah. As we approach Las Vegas, you'll be pleased that a temperature of one hundred ten degrees will only feel like one hundred," Craig teased.

Slowing down, Craig pointed out what looked like a coyote at the base of a mesa on their right. "I don't know if my depth perception is off, but whatever it is looks too small to be a coyote."

"I think it is a coyote," Steve affirmed. "But according to what I've read, the coyotes you're used to seeing in the Northeast have mated with the eastern Canadian red wolf and are much bigger—sometimes with a reddish coat."

"Interesting," Craig replied. "Speaking of wildlife, I'd like to see a jackrabbit but haven't seen any yet."

"I think they're mostly nocturnal," Steve said.

"Ah, that would explain it. There's an interesting book by Cormac McCarthy called *Cities of the Plains*. [xxvi] There's a passage in the book that has haunted me. Two ranch hands are driving their Oldsmobile at night in the high desert and keep hitting jackrabbits, who get frozen in the headlights—*blap! blap! blap!* They pull into a gas station at daylight before the days of self-service and wait for the attendant to finish filling up another car. Suddenly, a woman in the car being serviced begins screaming because the big, oval-shaped grille on the Oldsmobile is packed completely with jackrabbit heads. The jackrabbits had apparently turned their heads away just before impact so that the heads were all looking out of from the grille—

with what looked like a grin. As I read the passage, I wondered if it was a grin or a grimace."

Confused, Steve asked, "That's horrible. Is that your goal—hitting jackrabbits?"

"Good heavens no. I just want to see one," Craig answered.

"Okay. For a minute there, I thought you'd secretly ingested one of Duke's drug cocktails and gone over the edge."

"No. Duke and Gonzo experienced a number of hallucinations on their drive to and stay in Las Vegas, but according to the McCarthy story, the jackrabbit heads were real. Not something I'd want to experience," Craig said.

"I'm surprised that the Oldsmobile, with its air-cooled engine, didn't overheat with the grille completely blocked," Steve said.

"Good point. I seem to recall that the Oldsmobile did encounter an overheating problem, but the guys in the car shrugged it off, luckily getting to the gas station before the engine seized up."

"Speaking of dead rabbits," Steve said. "Do you ever ponder roadkill?"

"Only when I'm really hungry," Craig joked. "Talk about non-sequiturs."

"This may sound a little ghoulish," Steve offered, "but this past winter, I noticed a dead raccoon on the side of the road near our house. Roadkill usually disappears fairly quickly—either critters carry it away or the town clears it and tosses the carcass into an incinerator or compost bin. But in this particular instance, the dead raccoon remained in the same exact spot day after day."

"Okay," Craig said. "I can hardly wait for the punch line."

"There's no punch line," Steve said. "I just couldn't help observing the desecration of the body over time as cars kept running over it. At first, it was bodily fluids that dissipated. Then it was the viscera—followed by other soft tissue, including muscles. Then the bones. Over time, all that was left was skin and fur. Even that began to break up with little desiccated patches of fur sticking to the road—fighting the erasure of any evidence or even memory that the animal had even existed. Finally, even those patches disappeared. It troubled me greatly."

"You're weird, man," Craig laughed. "I can't say I've ever focused on roadkill before, probably because in Manhattan it would involve pedestrians."

"Maybe so," Steve conceded. "But I couldn't help but think of our own ephemeral existence on Earth. It's like those paperwhite narcissus that Tammy puts out in our kitchen to bloom in winter—unbelievably fragrant and evocative of spring and rebirth—but fleeting."

Craig grew quiet, pondering Steve's musings. For him, paperwhites smelled like dirty old socks. Nevertheless, the imagery of the raccoon and paperwhites struck a chord. He had often pondered what, if any, legacy he would leave to mark that he had ever lived.

As they drove on, Craig said, "Steve. See that side road coming up. Would you please slow down and pull onto the road?"

"Sure—but it's not much of a road," Steve replied. "If you want to take a piss, there's no traffic. We can just pull over."

"I have something else in mind," Craig said.

"Okay."

Noting that the gravel side road was turning to dirt, Steve asked, "What's up, Craig? This appears to be a road to nowhere."

"Pull up at the base of that rise just ahead."

Stepping out of the car and climbing to the top of the fifty foot rise, the two of them relieved themselves and marveled at the unobstructed views in all four directions.

"Steve, let me see your gun," Craig asked.

"Okay. It's a Glock 43X, which is the most popular handgun. It weighs under one and half pounds and is easily concealed. It's semi-automatic with a ten-round magazine and a 9mm gauge."

"May I hold it?"

"Yes—but be careful. There's no external safety; it shoots when you pull the trigger and is fairly sensitive."

Craig took the gun and found himself almost fondling it. "If feels good in my hand. It reminds me of the Beatles song 'Happiness is a Warm Gun' even though they had a different trigger in mind. [xxvii] Well balanced and lightweight—very ergonomic. I've never fired a gun before, but I can see why an enthusiast might like this one."

With that, Craig pointed the gun west and pulled the trigger—the sudden blast echoing on echoes.

Startled and reflexively ducking, Steve protested, "What in the hell are you doing?"

"Don't you remember Duke firing Gonzo's gun in the desert? I just wanted to try it. Duke fired in all four directions, but just like I'm not going to do drugs, I don't have to slavishly follow his example. I was prepared for a lot of 'kick-back.' This gun is smooth."

"Oh my God. It sounds like I've got a convert."

"Thanks, but no thanks. I just wanted to try it."

It was getting late in the afternoon, and the two of them pressed on into Nevada.

"I'm glad we drove this," Craig said. "But I don't want to drive back. It's just too much."

"I agree," Steve said.

***

Las Vegas is situated in the northeastern portion of the Mojave Desert in the rain shadow of the Sierra Nevada mountains. It's high desert with average elevations between twenty-five hundred and five thousand feet above sea level and can be cool at night in the winter. Contrary to popular belief, a desert is not a wasteland. Death Valley—located two hours from Las Vegas in the northern Mojave—the hottest, driest, lowest National Park in America—is a study in contrasts. Notwithstanding the highest temperature ever recorded on Earth, towering peaks are frosted with winter snow. Rare rainfall ushers in spectacular blooms of wildflowers from seeds that may have lain dormant for years. Lush oases support small fish and an abundance of diverse wildlife. Everything is not at it appears.

Craig took over for the last leg of the drive. As they drove on toward Las Vegas, Steve referenced a guidebook Craig had brought along to identify sage, creosote bushes, desert marigolds, Mojave aster, Joshua trees, yucca, cacti, succulents, and other desert vegetation. They were disappointed that the iconic Saguaro, the giant cactus that symbolizes the Sonoran Desert, is not native to the area. The guidebook noted that wildlife includes black bears, coyote, mountain lions, mule deer, bats, raccoons, rattlesnakes, any number of small mammals, and lizards— including the venomous Gila Monster. They were nowhere to be seen—at least not while the Red Shark barreled along at eighty miles per hour in the mid-day heat.

Getting closer to Las Vegas as the day began to fade, Steve suddenly gasped, "Oh my God. If I didn't know better, I'd say that's the Star of Bethlehem guiding us to our destination."

Slowing the car and pausing to study what Steve was seeing, Craig scoffed, "Nah. That's the Luxor Sky Beam atop the Luxor Hotel pyramid. It's the brightest light on Earth. I've read that it's visible from space and can be seen by pilots three hundred miles away. But like so much we'll experience in Las Vegas, up is down and down is up. The Star of Bethlehem came from the heavens and shone down on Earth, while the Luxor light comes from Earth and illuminates the heavens."

"I'm glad I'm not paying the electricity bill. I'll bet it could power a small town."

Laughing, Craig said, "You ain't seen nothing yet, Bro. Like trash-talking bloggers competing for social media followers, each casino flashes its most narcissistic selfies, screaming, 'Look at me!'"

Chapter 5
"Sin City"

It was dusk when they finally arrived in Las Vegas. Craig and Steve drove up "The Strip" bedazzled by the lights, crowds, and individual casinos mimicking carnival barkers, sex workers, and horny male birds fanning their tail feathers in an ostentatious "come-on."

As they pulled the Red Shark into the Bellagio to check in, the "Fountain Show," in a display the length of more than three football fields in the middle of the eight and half acre "Lagoon," erupted. Over one thousand fountains of water waved rhythmically in the air, with some jets of water shooting as high as four hundred-sixty feet, choreographed to pyrotechnics and, that evening, a Games of Thrones custom score using elements of the theme song and soundtrack.

Craig and Steve stood there mesmerized by the four-minute show—which occurs every fifteen or thirty minutes at certain times of day—as they turned their car keys over to a valet while a bellhop hustled their duffel bags and Steve's backpack inside. As they entered the lobby, their sensory perceptions, already slightly off-kilter, took another hit as they were bewitched by the *Fiori di Como,* the world's largest glass sculpture embedded in the ceiling, flashing more than two thousand colorful, hand-blown, glass flowers representing artist Dale Chihuly's interpretation of Italian flowers in spring.

"Keep your eye out for George Clooney and Brad Pitt," Steve joked. "I assume you know that *Ocean's Eleven* was filmed here."

"I do know that." Craig chuckled. "In fact, I think all three of the *Ocean's* trilogy were filmed at the Bellagio. However, I suspect that both George Clooney and Brad Pitt are at their villas on the real Lake Como as we speak."

As the two of them presented at the check-in counter, the "custom services representative," a very attractive young woman whose name tag identified her as "Dominique," cooed, "Welcome gentlemen. Mr. Wells, the manager of the Bellagio, Mr. Tobey Maguire, asked that I ping him the moment you arrived."

"Okay," Craig replied. "Dominique, while we wait for Mr. Maquire, would you please confirm our reservations at the 'Michael Mina' restaurant? The reservations were for six thirty, but we're already forty-five minutes late. I would appreciate it if we could move that time back to seven forty-five."

"Of course, Mr. Wells. I'll see what I can do."

The manager quickly appeared and fawned over them, gushing, "Mr. Wells. I've been looking forward to meeting you and your guest—Mr. Ehrlich, isn't it?"

Smiling as he reached out to shake hands, Craig said, "Mr. Wells was my dad. I'm Craig, and this is Steve."

"Thanks, Craig—and Steve. Please call me Tobey. I would like to comp your room, Mr. Wells—excuse me—Craig, and upgrade you to a suite."

"That's very nice of you, Tobey, but we prefer to stay with two queen size beds in one room. We plan to enjoy Las Vegas thoroughly and want to be each other's 'brother's keeper' while we're here."

"I understand completely. Craig, once again, I'm sorry I couldn't accommodate your request to use a jet ski on the lagoon. We only did it once, for Sir Richard Branson, to celebrate the tenth anniversary of Virgin Air's direct flight from London to Las Vegas. Unfortunately, Sir Richard, who was wearing a tuxedo, tipped the jet ski over and took a plunge. Both he and the flight attendant passenger came out soaking wet. Fortunately, no one was hurt, but our risk-management folks had a kitten about liability. One person actually drowned in broad daylight trying to swim out to the fountains. We've been very strict ever since. At this point, anyone entering the lagoon to swim or for any other reason—usually drunks—is not only ejected but forbidden from ever stepping on Bellagio property again. As we discussed, however, I can arrange for you to start the Fountain Show and select the music. You'll be seated at the VIP table at the Hyde Bellagio nightclub. You and your friends will be served a Midas-size, three foot tall, one hundred pound bottle of Jay Z's 'Ace of Spades' champagne, flanked by its own security team."

"Thanks, Tobey. If I recall, the price for the privilege is a quarter of a million dollars," Craig said.

"Yes. But you have to offset it against the cost of the champagne that typically sells for around one hundred fifty thousand dollars—plus tax and a tip," Maguire noted.

"I've heard about a 'Midas' bottle," Craig said. "Of course, in Greek mythology, Midas was a man who was granted his wish that everything he touched would turn into gold, not realizing that his wish was not a blessing but a curse. How much champagne does the bottle contain?"

"It's the equivalent of forty standard size bottles of champagne," Maguire said.

"As much as Steve and I intend to indulge—and even overindulge," Craig said laughing. "Forty bottles is a bit much even for us."

"Of course," Maguire replied, joining in the laughter. "It's more appropriate when you're hosting a large group."

After pausing for a minute, Maguire continued, "As we discussed on the phone, in the future you may want to stay in one of our villas. Each villa has a private butler service and private limousine entrance. You won't have to bother checking in at the front desk."

"Thanks, Tobey. I'll definitely consider that," Craig replied. "We want to visit the 'Viva Vision Light Show' on Fremont Street tomorrow evening. Can you arrange for a car?"

"Of course. Let me give you my cellphone number as well as the number of our dispatcher. Please feel free to summon a car at any time."

Dominique presented the key cards for their room and said, in a mellifluous voice, "All set on the room, gentlemen. Mr. Maguire, our guests had reservations at Michael Mina at six thirty this evening, but because of late arrival, they have requested moving that to seven forty-five. Unfortunately, the restaurant informs me that they don't have an opening."

"I'll take care of that," Maguire said. "Again, welcome to the Bellagio, Gentlemen. Please let me know if there's anything I can do for you during your stay."

"Thanks, Tobey. Much appreciated," Craig said, shaking hands while patting Tobey on his forearm.

Settling into their room, each showered eagerly after their dusty ride through the desert and changed into business casual.

"What did you say to the manager to get such royal treatment?" Steve asked.

"Nothing really, other than to ask about the jet skis. I suspect that such a privilege, if allowed, would have cost a pretty penny. He took it from there and inquired about my background. I mentioned my private equity fund—I could practically hear the cash register ringing in his head, 'ka-ching! ka-ching! ka-ching!' I suspect he identified me as a potential 'high roller' and wanted to woo me. Basically, in keeping with Las Vegas tradition, I showed him a little leg, and he got all hot and bothered."

"Cool. So—what kind of restaurant is Michael Mina?" Steve asked.

"There are ten Michelin-starred restaurants in Vegas. Money talks and Joël Robuchon, who, unfortunately, has passed, was lured from France and established the only three-star restaurant in Vegas called 'L'Atelier.' Robuchon has been considered the best chef of the modern age, with thirty-one stars for restaurants across three continents. L'Atelier means 'workshop' or 'studio' in

French. I suspect it was both to Robuchon. We've got reservations there tomorrow evening. Michael Mina is also French, a one-star seafood restaurant with fresh seafood flown in by private plane on a daily basis."

"You're not going to try and get me to eat escargot, are you?" Steve asked, laughing nervously.

"We'll go with the flow, Bro," Craig said, chuckling.

***

Michael Mina overlooks the Bellagio pool area with its classic Italian architecture containing five Mediterranean-inspired pools fed by Italian stone fountains set in a courtyard with lush gardens featuring cypress and citrus trees.

"Not bad," Steve said as the two of them strolled through the pool area on their way to the restaurant.

"Not bad indeed," Craig replied. "I have to give Steve Wynn credit. This setting transports me to Italy, one of my favorite places on Earth."

"I've never been," Steve said wistfully.

Smiling, Craig declared, "You're there now. In addition to Lake Como, you can visit the most famous attractions of Rome at Caesar's Palace, including replicas of the Colosseum and Casa di Augusto, the home of Emperor Augustus Octavius Caesar. You can find yourself on the Grand Canal, cross the Rialto Bridge, visit St. Mark's Campanile, and see the Piazza San Marco at the Venetian. There's even a small Italian village just outside the city called 'Aston MonteLago Village' with cobblestone streets, historic-looking buildings, fountains, and shops. Like Vegas itself, each represents altered reality."

"I hear you Craig, but I must admit that I envy your travel to see the real deal," Steve said.

Pausing for a moment, Craig asked, "Do you remember the first time you had sex? I'll never forget mine—it was like nothing I'd ever experienced before and opened a whole new world for me. I'll let you in on a little secret. Travel is like sex. I'm not knocking it because it's still fun, but after a while it's sorta like, 'Been there, done that.'"

"I'm beginning to understand your reference to the 'beige blur,'" Steve observed. "As for me, of course I remember the first time. I was in high school. A classmate of mine named Becky Thompson and I hooked up in the woods behind her house. It was mind-blowing. I was so excited I came almost instantly. It was embarrassing. With Tammy, the experience was transcendent. This probably sounds cliché, but I guess it was the difference between having sex and making love. The dopamine hits kept coming, but there was more. I can't really describe it. It was like a different dimension shared by just the two of us. I was always happy and content to be in her presence."

"You were horny, Bro." Craig laughed.

"Yeah," Steve acknowledged, "but it was more than that. We had climbed to the top of the mountain, and the world was at our feet. Now, all I can think of is B.B. King's song: 'The Thrill is Gone,' or hear Gordon

Lightfoot singing mournfully 'If You Could Read My Mind.' [xxviii] It makes me want to cry."

"I envy you, Steve. I never got to the top of the mountain. I suspect very few people have."

"But I think you can sense it, Craig. Your earlier comments about kissing under a meteor shower showed your cards."

"Maybe; maybe not," Craig mused. "As to you, I think you should do everything you can to claw your way back up."

Peering into Steve's eyes and reading his profound sense of loss and bewilderment, Craig went into default mode. "I need a drink. How about you?"

"Do you really have to ask?"

Their waiter was from Central Casting—an Italian from Naples named "Gio." He was rakishly handsome and carried himself with a certain 'je ne sais quoi.'

"Gio, what's the signature drink of the Bellagio?" Craig asked.

"It's the 'Tango Cocktail," Gio enthused. "We use a citrus-forward gin mixed with grapefruit juice softened by a sweet Passoa Passionfruit Liquer."

"Sold!" Craig said. "We'll take two."

Craig and Steve pored over the menu, waiting for their drinks to appear.

"I see they have 'Portuguese' octopus, Steve. Want to try a different version?"

"I liked the octopus last night, but—this will probably surprise you—I'm feeling even more adventurous. Let's try something different—something I'll never get back home."

Gio returned with their Tangos, and each took a sip.

"Delizioso!" Craig said, toasting the waiter. "Gio— just a heads-up. We have tickets for the nine-thirty Cirque du Soleil 'O' show. I hate to hurry what I'm sure will be a wonderful dining experience, but wanted to let you know we have limited time. Our original reservation was for six-thirty, but unfortunately, we got delayed. What do you recommend from the chef tonight?"

"We'll make sure to have you out of here by nine-thirty. The Royal Osetra is spectacular," Gio said. "I also love the foie gras, a combination of Pacific and Atlantic oysters, the Perigord black truffle risotto, the phyllo-crusted Petrale Sole, and the roasted magic mushrooms."

"Wait a minute," Craig said with a glint of mischief in his eye. "Magic mushrooms? Are they what I think they are?"

Laughing, Gio said, "No truth in advertising. No, they're not what you think—no hallucinogenic properties. But delicious. Unlike any mushrooms you've ever tried."

"What's Petrale Sole?" Steve asked.

"Gio, let me take this one," Craig interjected. "The Petrale Sole isn't actually sole at all; rather, it's a right eyed flounder. As I understand it, the fish is called a 'sole' because it's more marketable. It's only found in the Pacific. It's delicious."

"I'm sorry," Steve said. "What do you mean that it's 'right eyed?'"

Gio chimed in, "Flat fish start out as normal fish, with eyes on both sides of their bodies. As they mature, the bones on one side of their skull grow faster than the other so that one eye and nostril slowly migrate to the other side and their body flattens. In the case of the Petrale Sole, both eyes end up on the right side of the fish, and they lie on the bottom on their left side. The flat shape allows them to hide under the sand with only their eyes protruding, periscope-like, which allows them to be expert 'ambush' predators."

"I think flatfish are the most delicate and tasty of all fish, and the Petrale is the best of the best," Craig said.

"Okay," Steve replied. "Sounds weird, but I'll take your word for it. I'm used to channel catfish, which is the state fish of Missouri, or 'lake white fish' from the Great Lakes, but I'll give the Petrale a try. Tell me about foie gras. Isn't it duck or goose liver?"

"Wait a minute—there's a state fish in Missouri?" Craig asked, laughing. "Once again, I'm impressed with the heavy duty policy making going on in state legislatures. As to foie gras, it's banned in parts of the United States because the goose or duck is force-fed to fatten the liver. But it's absolutely heavenly: rich, buttery, and delicate. Gio, let's do all of your recommendations."

"We can't possible eat all that, can we?" Steve asked.

"Probably not, but as our theme this week is, 'If it's good enough to do, it's good enough to overdue,' let's give it a try," Craig said, laughing.

"Very good, sir. Do you want to continue with the Tangos or switch to wine?"

"Let's have a bottle of your best white Burgundy and go from there. What do you recommend, Gio?"

"As I'm sure you know, some of the white Burgandies are among the best and highest priced wines in the world. Personally, I like the modestly-priced Louis Jadot 2020 Puligny-Montrachet. It has heavenly aromas of toasted hazelnuts, almonds, and vanilla, along with fruit scents and flavors of lemon zest, lemon custard, and Granny Smith apples. It would complement your meal perfectly."

"What does 'modestly-priced' mean?" Steve asked.

"We'll take it, Gio," Craig said.

As Gio left to place their order, Steve said with a pained look, "As daring as I'm trying to be experimenting with food, the foie gras and oysters might be a challenge for me."

"That's cool, Bro," Craig replied reassuringly. "I don't know if you noticed, but the foie gras is from the Hudson River Valley in New York State. That area introduced the delicacy to the American palate a little over thirty years ago. Ironically, New York City, California, and other places like Chicago banned it because of protests by PETA and other animal rights advocates alleging cruelty. Hell, you can 'force-feed' me foie gras all day. By the way, Chicago's ban has since been rescinded. I was actually in Chicago at a restaurant the day before the ban went into effect back in—I think it was around 2006. The chef served copious amounts of foie gras 'gratis' that night to clear out his supply. It was a wonderful windfall."

"I notice it isn't gratis here," Steve said, laughing. "And the price of the caviar is close to my monthly mortgage. I'm glad you're paying."

"My pleasure, Bro."

The food was superb, as was the service. Steve even liked the caviar and foie gras. Much to Craig's amusement, Steve gagged on his second attempt to slurp an oyster and bailed on a third.

"My God," Steve said. "I like being adventuresome, but the texture of oysters is like rubber bands in snot."

Craig just laughed as he slurped away.

They had time for dessert and ordered the "Textures of Chocolate" offering consisting of cocoa chiffon, milk chocolate pot de crème, and burnt caramel ice cream— with a wine pairing.

Steve whispered to Craig, "Although the dessert is fantastic, the prices across the board are mind blowing."

"Welcome to Las Vegas," Craig said, laughing.

***

The performance was being held at the Bellagio's theater and aquatic stage with its giant, one and half million gallon, twenty-five-foot deep swimming pool. The venue was designed and constructed when the Bellagio was being built specifically for the Cirque du Soleil "O" show. It includes a massive carousel in the rafters that lowers and lifts performers and props; a segmented stage that can change heights; and a sophisticated light and sound room.

As the two of them settled into their lower orchestra front row seats, fresh Tango Cocktails in hand, Craig whispered, "I knew it would be a long day, Steve, which is why I opted for the 'O' show here at the Bellagio. I hope you don't mind."

"I'm delighted," Steve responded. "I'm tired and would love to get a good night's sleep."

"I do have one request," Craig said. "I know we agreed to sleep until noon each day while we're here, but tomorrow morning I'd like to get to the Craps tables early. The players are most interesting at that time, having been up all night or wandered in early. They each have a unique story—even if they're reluctant to talk about it. It's fun to tease out those stories or draw conclusions based on clues they drop."

"Urggh!" Steve growled. "I really do want to sleep in."

"This show will be over by eleven. That's the tradeoff—it's almost certainly the earliest we'll be in."

"Okay, Craig. But no more early mornings! Based on how much alcohol we've already consumed and how much more appears to be in our immediate future, I'll need time to recover."

"Sounds like a plan, Bro," Craig said as he toasted Steve and took a sip of his cocktail. "As to alcohol, we'll hook you up to a daily IV for hydration if necessary," Craig joked.

The "O" show was a revelation to both of them. As they soon discovered, the theme is that of a boy on a mesmerizing journey into a mysterious aquatic world.

Craig and Steve had each been to a traveling circus with acrobats under the big top when they were kids. This, however, was NOT your father's Oldsmobile—nor Carmac McCarthy's. There was one jaw-dropping performance after another, all enhanced by augmented reality, including lighting, sound, a moving stage, and countless optical illusions. A spectral boat floated above the mist, manned by a ghostly crew. Fire engulfed the pool. Performers appeared to walk on water. There was surreal underwater dancing. The show was a mix of creativity, athleticism, and special effects, inducing a dreamlike experience that would astonish even the most jaded.

The two were blown away and sat in their seats for a few minutes processing what they had witnessed after the show ended.

Steve enthused, "Wow! That was absolutely incredible. I'm having even more trouble digesting what we just experienced than those oysters."

Laughing, Craig said, "I'll say it again. Welcome to Las Vegas."

As they departed the aquatic stage, Craig mentioned that the "O" show has been performed only at the Bellagio since its opening in 1998.

"Understandable since the brochure indicates that the theater and pool were designed specifically for the show," Steve said. "In this case, I think it's fair to say that 'What happens in Las Vegas stays in Las Vegas.'"

"Actually," Craig observed. "It represents just the opposite. As we've discussed, at this point 'What happens in Las Vegas' becomes mainstream for the rest of the country. You know the old adage from Napoleon Hill: 'Whatever the mind of man can conceive and believe, it can achieve.' There's already a twelve minute, three hundred sixty-degree, 3D, immersive VR video called 'Dreams of O' that is an abridged version of the show that may have already been accessed by your kids."

"Unreal," Steve sighed.

***

Before retiring to their room, Craig suggested they take in the Fountain Show one more time before calling it a night. They decided to view the show from a different vantage point down next to the lagoon. As all eyes turned to the water and light extravaganza, Craig peed discreetly into the lagoon while finishing a Tango cocktail he had brought along.

"Oh my God, Bro. Are you crazy? You're going to get us arrested—or banned from the Bellagio," Steve protested.

Laughing, Craig said, "Nature called. Besides, I'm just doing my part to replenish the water in the lagoon that evaporates so quickly here in the desert."

"I don't think Sir Richard Branson or Tobey would appreciate your gesture—as well-meaning as it is," Steve replied as he burst into laughter and relieved himself.

"I must admit," Craig said, laughing giddily. "I'm not quite as eager to use a jet ski on the lagoon at this point."

Back in their room, Craig asked, "Do you want a nightcap from the mini-bar?"

"No thanks," Steve said. "If I have one more drink, I think I'll spend the rest of the night running to the toilet upchucking. I just need to crash."

"Okay, Bro. Did you call Tammy earlier?"

"When was I going to do that?" Steve answered.

"Oh, I don't know—maybe when I was in the shower."

"There just wasn't time," Steve responded, showing a flash of irritation. "I texted her that we arrived safely. I told you I would call her, and I will. Stop bugging me."

"Just thinking of you, Steve."

"Good night, Craig."

Chapter 6
Craps, Chocolate, and Distorted Reality

"Come on, Steve. Wake up."

Pulling the covers over his head, Steve groaned, "I thought our deal was sleeping until noon and partying all night. I have a pounding headache and just want to stay in bed."

"I think you'll enjoy this," Craig cajoled. "As I told you last night, the people at the Craps Tables in the morning are the most interesting because most of them have been there all night. It makes you wonder why. It's fascinating to try and figure out their individual stories."

"No thanks. You can share your observations with me later."

"I promise you—this will be worth it," Craig implored.

Reluctantly pulling the covers down below his eyes and peeking out, Steve whined, "I don't even know what Craps is about—other than that people roll dice. Why in hell is it called 'Craps' in the first place?"

"From what I understand, the word is a bastardization of the French word 'crapaud,' which means 'toad,'" Craig replied. "It refers to the original style of play by people crouched over a floor or sidewalk."

Grudgingly rousing himself, Steve sat for a moment on the side of his bed. He looked like he had been dragged backwards through a hedge with hair all askew and gray stubble sprouting on his face like the prickles on a wild thistle. Finally, he reluctantly agreed.

"Speaking of 'Craps,' let me take a dump, shave, and hop in the shower. I reserve the right to take a nap when we get back."

"Fair enough," Craig said.

Twenty minutes later, both were dressed in jeans, gym shoes, and long-sleeve T-shirts—the latter being a concession to the AC that gets ramped up in a casino to keep people from feeling sleepy. Because it's a luxury resort, there is a dress code for restaurants and clubs at the Bellagio, but the gaming areas are fairly relaxed when it comes to attire unless something offensive is being worn.

"I know you've never played Craps before, Steve. The object of the game is straightforward enough: correctly predicting the outcome of the roll of two dice. But it's more complicated than that."

Rolling his eyes, Steve said, "Why am I not surprised?"

"I've only played a couple of times," Craig said, "and I must admit, it's confusing for a newcomer as well as somewhat intimidating because of all the casino people involved. There's a 'boxman,' who oversees everything and settles disputes, counts the money, and makes sure things are running smoothly. There are also four 'dealers.' A dealer would be called a 'croupier' at a roulette table. One dealer is out on a rotating twenty minute break at all times; the three dealers present take turns being the 'stickman,' who handles the dice with a flexible wooden stick. The dealers keep track of bets, pay you if you win, and take chips if you lose. They also place certain types of bets for you."

"Doesn't sound straightforward to me," Steve shot back. "And, as you explain more, I suspect it's only going to get more complicated."

"I have to admit that I'm just touching the surface with the little I know. In addition to the rules, even though Craps is supposedly a game of pure chance and not strategy, in talking with the players, I've observed that they each have their own angles on betting to lower the casino's odds. Statistically, the dice land on certain number combinations with different probabilities. The higher the probability, the lower the amount of payout."

"Are you kidding me? It sounds like learning about IT without a twelve year old helping," Steve said with an exasperated sigh.

Laughing, Craig said, "Yeah. That's a fair assessment." Tongue firmly in cheek, he quipped, "Too bad we didn't think to bring your daughter, Jennifer, with us."

"I'm sure she would have loved the Tango Cocktails," Steve snickered.

"There are certain things that make Craps the most fun—at least for me," Craig enthused. "For one thing, unlike other casino games, the boxman and dealers are actually rooting for you to win because they're normally awarded a 'tip' of up to twenty percent of winnings, which they split. Secondly, unlike poker, where you have a lot of very serious, almost grim, people sitting at the table wearing sunglasses and hoods pulled up to hide any physical 'tells,' in Craps there's usually a festive mood with drinking, socializing, and even a lot of good-natured shouting with as many as twenty players. Third, the house odds, while not as low as blackjack, are pretty low. Fourth, the players who roll the dice, the so-called 'shooters,' really get everyone into the game emotionally with their individual idiosyncrasies and flair. Finally, although you can double your money in a relatively short period of time playing blackjack, a winner in Craps can go from five grand to half a million dollars in that same amount of time. For many people, it's the chance to catch the American Dream."

"But how in the hell do you bet and win?" Steve asked.

"Frankly, that's where it gets difficult for me because there are so many types of bets. As a beginner, I just do so-called 'Pass Line' bets for 'even money' where you win if a seven or eleven roll, or lose if a two, three, or twelve turn up. If any other number appears, the dice have to be rolled again. I'm oversimplifying, but it's the most popular bet because it's straightforward and the house odds are relatively low."

"What does 'even money' mean?" Steve asked.

"If you bet, for example, one hundred dollars—you win one hundred dollars," Craig said.

"And there are more complex bets?" Steve protested. "Why am I getting the feeling that betting in Craps is as easy as using a slide rule in chemistry class—something I tried as a student but could never figure out?"

Laughing again, Craig said, "Just observe at first. Hell, I understand that it takes twelve to fourteen weeks to train a dealer. Neither of us will pick up all of the nuances, but you'll see—it's fun."

"I'll take your word for it," Steve said. "But right now, I need a super-sized cup of black coffee."

As they walked into the gaming rooms, Steve hesitated and whispered to Craig, "Man, this place smells like stale beer and cigarette butts floating in unfinished drinks. There's also the metallic smell of day-old perfume as well as body odor. It reminds me of the morning after a party at our house when Tammy and I have gone to bed without cleaning up."

"I don't know when the cleaning crews cycle through this place," Craig said. "A lot of the players have been here all night, and no matter how good housekeeping is, they can't do much about people. The good news is that we'll become inured to it after a while, and all we'll smell is the refreshing citrus and other scents the casino pumps in."

Bracing themselves, they joined a boisterous group at one of the Craps tables. As is typical in all of the casinos, the gaming areas have no windows or natural light and no clocks—which is intentional to confuse players as to what time it is and keep them engaged no matter what the hour. The ceilings are blacked out to keep the focus on the gambling.

Craig bought into the game and stepped up to the table while Steve hung back and observed.

Craig positioned himself next to the only woman among the twenty players at the table. She was a tall, lithe blond about his age—dressed in a stylish black split hem halter and wide leg trousers that contrasted jarringly from the others, who looked pretty ratty in general with an assortment of T-shirts, light hoodies, and loose-fitting floral shirts.

"Hi. I'm Craig Wells. I'm visiting from Manhattan and am a rank amateur at Craps. Any insights would be appreciated."

"Hi Craig. The regulars call me 'Paradise' because that's where I live."

"Fantastic." Craig chuckled. "We all want to live in paradise."

"Maybe, maybe not," Paradise snickered. "In this case, it's the name of the unincorporated town next to Vegas that hosts most of the Strip, including the Bellagio."

"Ah," Craig laughed. "The blood clot just moved in my brain, and I get it. Nice to meet you, Paradise."

"Nice to meet you as well," Paradise responded.

"Paradise, I couldn't help but notice that you're the only woman at the table. Is that the norm?"

"At this time of the morning, it is. I like to play with all men because they 'mansplain' Craps to me, assuming that a 'girl' couldn't possibly know how to play."

"In my case, the tables are turned—pun intended—because I can use any kind of 'splaining' I can get since I'm a beginner," Craig said. "If you don't mind, I'll lean on you for any tips."

"No problem," Paradise replied with a big smile. "It'll be a nice change of pace."

The current "shooter" turned out to be a character. He had a physical disability and was perched on a lightweight Tri-pod stool that could be folded and easily transported.

Speaking to Craig in a hushed tone, Paradise said, "The shooter's nickname is 'Knock-Knock' because he raps his knuckles on his throwing hand twice on the railing before rolling the dice. He's always dressed the same, including that beat-up baseball cap with the gold logo shouting to the world that he's a 'Vet.'"

Studying Knock-Knock, Craig observed that his hands had so many "age spots" that, although it might have been possible to connect the dots at some point, the spots had merged together creating a brown patina that contrasted markedly with the vascular rosacea on the cheeks of his light-skinned face. Craig assumed he was a heavy drinker.

Leaning in close to Craig, Paradise whispered, "Knock-Knock is always here. I'm not sure he has anywhere else to go."

"Damn," Paradise said, observing a roll of the dice. "Another ballerina."

"Excuse me?" Craig asked. "What's a ballerina?"

"It's two twos, but sounds like 'tutu' and thus the name 'ballerina.'"

"I get it," Craig said. "It's like 'snake eyes' for two ones."

"Exactly," Paradise chirped. "Two sixes is a 'Columbian breakfast' because of the two lines on each of the dice. Two fives is a 'pair of sunflowers,' and so on.

"Got it," Craig said.

Much to his consternation, Knock-Knock rolled Craps and passed the baton, with Craig becoming the shooter. As he started to pick up the dice, Paradise leaned in once again and whispered, "Let me 'womansplain' something to you. Never use the dice from a bad roll. Insist on new ones."

"Okay," Craig replied.

As he retrieved the new dice, he started to blow on them before rolling—something he had once seen in a movie.

Paradise whispered, "That's a 'no-no' Craig. The dice can't be wet, and consequently blowing on them is a breach of Craps etiquette."

Observing and overhearing Paradise's comment, Steve thought to himself— *there's such a thing as "Craps etiquette?" Who knew?*

Craig rolled a three, with players betting the "Pass Line" groaning "Craps" because they lost.

Craig ceded the role of shooter to Paradise to the delight of many of the regulars because they regarded her as a lucky charm. In fact, she told Craig that the players often tipped her on a winning roll. One could feel the anticipation rising at the table—including among the dealers—as the constant "buzz" ramped up a couple of octaves.

As Paradise stepped into the white-hot spotlight, she paused as if she were meditating while cupping the dice in her hands. Rolling a seven with a backspin flair, she was transformed, yelling "Yes" while pumping her fist in the air. She then pranced like a singer performing on stage—to the cheers of her fans. As she kept rolling winner after winner, all Craig could compare the scene to was Tina Turner or Mick Jagger strutting at the peak of one of their lathered performances.

The "Rolling Stones" song "Gimme Shelter" screamed in Craig's head. [xxix] The haunting opening riff—which grabs you by the lapels and demands your full attention. The singular voice of Merry Clayton sending chills up your spine as it rises in an ever-ascending scale of urgency. The song building tension like a runaway freight train heading off a cliff.

And like the anti-war song, the inevitable crash came when Paradise rolled "Craps" and bowed out as shooter—totally spent—glistening with sweat.

Giving Paradise a moment as she cooled down, Craig was concerned enough to offer getting her a drink of water, but she declined.

"I'll be okay," Paradise said. "All I can compare this moment to is dopamine levels dropping below baseline after an orgasm."

Startled by Paradise's frank description while plumbing the archives of his brain for a fact check, he finally said, "Understood. I guess the other analogy is taking 'downers' after 'uppers.'"

There was no response from Paradise, as she appeared to be drained.

Craig continued, "I was wondering why you're wearing a halter top when my friend and I wore long sleeves in case the AC got too cold."

Smiling, Paradise said, "As you can see—clearly not a problem when I'm rolling because it's such a rush. It's also not a problem at other times because of the scourge of 'hot flashes.' Men have no idea how lucky they are."

Turning to look at Craig, she laughed and said, "Yes. I'm at that stage in my life. Not a lot of fun."

Craig chuckled but held his tongue.

Steve had stepped away during Paradise's winning run to fetch refreshments. He appeared with a fresh draft Guinness Stout for Craig along with one for himself as he kidded, "Why a Guinness? I was reminded of an old Guinness advertisement: 'Not just for breakfast anymore.'"

Laughing, Craig took a sip and placed the beer on the railing of the Craps table. He was quietly scolded by Paradise, who had already moved past her "refractory" period, ready for another go, "The railing is for chips, not for food or drinks. Hold the drink in your hand—the one you don't use if you're rolling."

"Okay," Craig replied as he quickly complied with her instructions.

A couple of the players—obviously friends who appeared to have been up all night drinking—were high-fiving with a win, drooping to an almost catatonic state with a loss. One wore an ill-fitting Hawaiian shirt that still had the price tag attached. No one had the heart to mention it. The other wore a Las Vegas T-shirt that proudly proclaimed, "One casino; Two casino; Three casino; Poor." Based on how badly they fared, the slogan appeared to be a fitting description of their time playing Craps in Las Vegas. Craig assumed both were tourists and not regulars.

One of the regulars was called "Four Eyes" because of his thick eyeglasses. The name could have been offensive, but Four-Eyes took it in stride—and perhaps even pride—as a form of affection. He was a short, balding, non-descript man who, if he had been wearing a green eyeshade, would have been a perfect caricature of the low-ranking accountant in the last cubicle. Craig wondered if the nickname was a badge of honor—one of the few times in his life that he had been singled out for distinction.

Turning back to Paradise, he asked, "What do you do for living?"

Paradise hesitated, but then said, "The regulars—myself included—use nicknames because we keep our lives separate from the Craps table not wanting to punctuate fantasy with reality."

"I respect that," Craig said. "On the other hand, I'm just visiting with my friend. Not much chance that our lives will intersect outside the casino."

"Okay," Paradise said. "I work three, twelve hour shifts a week as an X-ray technician at Summerlin Hospital Medical Center. I'm divorced without a family, and playing Craps several mornings each week is my major outlet. I'm actually pretty good at it and, on balance, make a few bucks from time to time. Not much, but it's the adrenaline, escapism, sense of belonging, sheer fun, and—I must admit—the release I get when winning and starring as the shooter, rather than the money, that keeps me coming."

"What if you struck it big, which I understand you can do in Craps? How would that change your life?"

"I can dream. I've often thought of all I might do with a lot of money. I swing wildly among quitting my job, traveling, moving out of the desert to Hawaii or one of the Coasts, being a philanthropist, and on and on. It's a fun fantasy, but in all truthfulness, I'm not sure I would change anything other than the size of my bets. My job keeps me grounded, and playing Craps gives me mindless pleasure. And of course, the chance of ever hitting it big is a fantasy with odds only slightly better than all those people—including me—who buy lottery tickets."

"Great perspective!" Craig said. "How about regulars like 'Knock-Knock' or 'Four Eyes?' What are their stories?"

"There is a camaraderie at the Craps table, but I have no idea what their real lives are like. To be honest, I feel sorry for a lot of the regulars. I don't probe, but my sense is that they're either addicted to the endorphin and dopamine hits associated with winning—or don't have much else in their lives—or both. Why else would they stay up all night playing? I don't get here until eight or nine in the morning. Most of these guys have been here for hours."

"Based on their thousand-yard stares while not winning—only coming to life while on a roll—I think you're spot on," Craig said. "In fact, as I think about it, all I compare it to is what I imagine to be a Narcan revival after a heroin overdose."

"Interesting comparison," Paradise observed. "I have a friend who is hooked on one-arm bandits. The flashing lights, vivid colors, immersive graphics, arcade sounds—and the thrill of coming 'oh so close' to winning time and time again as all the oranges almost align—or even small wins keeping hope alive for the jackpot just around the corner. She's in Gamblers Anonymous but lapses time and time again."

Chuckling, Paradise continued, "It's like a guy I met at a bar who told me that giving up alcohol is no big deal—he does it all the time. As for me, I'm very strict at setting limits on how much I can afford to lose and how long I'll play."

"Good for you," Craig said. "I'm blown away by claims from casino owners that it's not the slot machines that cause addiction, but rather the people themselves. Sounds a lot like the line from the NRA."

"I hadn't thought of it that way," Paradise said. "I guess both are true."

Putting his arm around Steve and pulling him up to the table, Craig said, "Let me introduce you to my friend."

"Steve, meet Paradise. As you can clearly see, Paradise is the 'belle of the ball' at this Craps table."

Paradise chirped, "Pretty easy to do when you're the only woman at the ball. Nice to meet you Steve. Are you going to take a turn?"

"Nice to meet you as well, Paradise. Sure. I'd like to be the shooter at least once."

With that, Steve took over Craig's position and got an opportunity to roll. He did it with such exuberance that rather than simply bouncing off the back wall of the Craps table, the dice flew off the table and scattered on the floor. Everyone groaned, and Steve was embarrassed. The dealer replaced the dice, and Steve rolled again—this time successfully—although he "crapped out," eliciting more groans.

"Something tells me that this is not a game I'm going to master." Steve chuckled.

"Don't feel bad," Paradise said. "Believe it or not, it takes hours to learn how to roll the dice properly."

"Learning how to roll; how to place bets; how to play the odds; I'm even more convinced that this is not a game for me—too much work," Steve said with a staccato laugh that sounded vaguely like the ragged *rat-a-tat-tat* of a woodpecker who had experimented with too many fermented crab apples.

"Damn," Craig whispered to Steve. "There's that pre-pubescent cackle again."

"Thanks, Pal," Steve retorted while "cackling" with abandon.

Looking at Steve, Paradise mused, "I wonder if your attitude would change if you got on a winning roll."

"I wonder as well," Craig said. "Unfortunately, we don't have time to test that hypothesis because we have to split. Paradise, it's been nice meeting you. Thanks for the 'womansplaining.' Good luck on hitting it big!"

"Nice to meet both of you. Good luck to you as well," Paradise replied with a quick flash of a smile—her attention immediately drawn back inexorably to the action.

As they exited, Steve declared emphatically, "Now I want my nap."

"Not yet, Steve. I have something else in mind. There's somewhere I want to take you. Let's ask the valet to bring the Red Shark around."

"Promises, Promises!" Steve said in feigned disappointment. "Okay, but I'm sleeping into tomorrow no matter what."

***

As Craig drove the Red Shark out of the Bellagio, Steve asked, "Where are we going?"

"It's a surprise, but we're going to see a bit of the country."

It was just before noon, and the day was heating up quickly. They put the ragtop up to get a little relief from the sun, but there was no AC and the vinyl seats felt like heating pads on their backs. The idea of long sleeve T-shirts now appeared to be a gross miscalculation.

"Man, I don't know what we were thinking scheduling this trip for July," Steve said. "It's the hottest time of the year in one of the hottest places in the country."

"Yeah. Not the best planning on my part, but you're off from school in the summer, and I was able to find some time," Craig said.

As they drove to exit the Strip, Steve asked in wonderment, "Boy, the roads around here are all under construction. I don't think I've ever seen so many orange cones. I wonder what's going on."

"I read somewhere that a 'Grand Prix' race course is being built down Las Vegas Boulevard and around The Strip."

"Do you mean 'Grand Prix' like in Monaco?" Steve asked.

"That's what I understand. If I recall correctly, over half a billion dollars is being spent to get the course ready for November with repaved streets, temporary bridges, outdoor grandstands for eighteen thousand people, and the largest 'Formula One' facility in the world—the length of three football fields located behind the Planet Hollywood resort with exclusive clubs, a huge video screen, and skyboxes. It's so Las Vegas."

"Unbelievable. Just what Las Vegas needs—more entertainment!" Steve said.

"Yeah. And now the Oakland A's are moving to town, just like the Oakland Raiders did a couple of years ago," Craig said. "The legendary Tropicana is being demolished for a one and half billion dollar ballpark. The area keeps growing and growing. I just read that a private company has received approval to develop the first bullet train in America. It will travel the two hundred-fifteen mile distance from Los Angeles to Las Vegas at two hundred miles per hour. The project is projected to cost at least twelve billion dollars, will apparently start this year, and will be done by 2027. You have to wonder if all this building is sustainable."

"Mind boggling!" Steve exclaimed.

A little less than an hour later, they pulled into the town of Pahrump—about sixty miles west of Las Vegas and close to Death Valley National Park, which is just over the border in California.

"Okay," Steve said. "Why are we in Pahrump? And what kind of a name is that?"

Laughing, Craig said, "It's still a surprise, Bro. My guidebooks tell me that the town's name comes from the Southern Pauite words 'Pah-Rimpi,' which means 'Water Rock' because of the abundance of artesian wells in the area. The area originally had a number of large ranches that grew alfalfa and cotton. They raised livestock too. With the draining of the surface aquifers, most agriculture has disappeared."

"Not surprising," Steve said. "Aquifers have to be replenished—sometimes taking thousands of years in a dry climate like this—and digging deeper and deeper to find water simply postpones the inevitable."

"I'm afraid that's true," Craig said. "I read somewhere that twelve million gallons of water evaporates each year from the Bellagio Fountains and Lagoon. Talk about wasteful and mindless excess."

Craig continued, "When we're in downtown Las Vegas tonight, one of the famous old-style casinos we'll visit is Binion's. The son of the founder of the casino, Ted

Binion, buried a large treasure of silver in a secret underground vault here in Pahrump. Back in 1998, he died under suspicious circumstances. One of the people accused of murdering Binion was apprehended while trying to dig up the vault. There's a book, *Positively Fifth Street* by James McManus, that delves into the subsequent murder trial and the game of poker, which is inextricably tied to Binion's, the original site of the 'World Series of Poker.'" [xxx] Not unlike Duke, McManus was in Las Vegas on assignment. *Harper's Magazine* commissioned McManus to cover the murder trial. He entered the poker tournament while here and finished fifth. The book is a fascinating memoir describing both the trial and the poker tournament."

"How in the hell do you know all this?" Steve asked. "By the way, I haven't read the book, but I seem to remember a Bob Dylan song with a similar title."

"I always read lots of guidebooks before traveling. I've found that if you don't research a destination, you may miss the highlights. Seeing the reference to McManus' book, I read it. It provides some invaluable insights into Las Vegas. And you're correct, the title to the book was inspired by Dylan's 'Positively Fourth Street.' [xxxi] Google the lyrics and you'll understand why. I'll put the book on your reading list, Professor Ehrlich."

"Since Tammy and I never travel anywhere, we just haven't gotten into the habit of reading guidebooks. Even if we did, I suspect Pahrump wouldn't be on our bucket list."

"I've been craving some authentic Mexican food—not TexMex," Craig enthused. "There's apparently a great place here called 'El Jefe's.' It's just up the road."

"Sounds good," Steve said. "But surely we didn't drive sixty miles in this heat for Mex."

Laughing, Craig said, "Be patient, my friend. The surprise awaits us."

The two of them grabbed a booth at El Jefe's. The waitress, whose name was 'Rosa,' greeted them with a warm smile. "Can I get you guys a drink?" she asked with a heavy Spanish accent—adding a note of authenticity to the restaurant's reputation.

"I'm parched," Craig said, laughing. "How about you, Steve?"

"You bet."

"How about bringing us a couple of margaritas, with salt, Rosa. And two large glasses of ice water," Craig requested.

"My pleasure," Rosa replied as she quickly pivoted. Although attentive, efficient, and engaging, she was working a half-dozen tables, including one with a boisterous family of ten, and was slammed. The family, which appeared to be Hispanic, was celebrating the birthday of one of the boys. When the birthday cake was presented, the boy blew out the candles, and the wait staff joined in the festive mood, singing "Happy Birthday."

As Rosa returned with their drinks along with chips and salsa, Craig asked if the guidebook he'd read about the restaurant serving genuine Mexican food was accurate.

"Si," Rosa replied. "My family is from Guanajuato, Mexico, and I can personally vouch for the authenticity."

"How about the chips and salsa?" Craig asked. "I've read that they're more TexMex than Mex. Are chips and salsa popular in Mexico?"

"Not really," she replied. "We're more likely to have potato chips smothered in Valentina and lime."

"What's Valentina?" Steve asked.

"It's a very popular hot sauce," Rosa replied.

"I guess chips and salsa are comparable to a dish like Fettucine Alfredo, which is popular in Italian-American restaurants but not found in Italy," Craig observed. "Rosa, do you have any tacos with special fillings that we don't often see in the U.S.?"

"Si," she replied. "In addition to traditional fillings like Carne Asada, Al Pastor and Carnitas pork, there's also a taco made with goat meat and another made with beef tongue."

"If it's okay with you, Steve, we'll take two each of the goat meat and beef tongue," Craig replied.

"What the hell. Why not?" Steve said as he quickly finished his drink. "And Rosa—two more margaritas please."

As Rosa hustled their order to the kitchen, Steve said: "Okay. I tried that Korean/Mexican burrito with kimchi, tofu, and that awful Korean sauce. I guess I'm willing to try anything. Tammy will be surprised at how fearless I've become with food. I'm basically a 'regular' meat and potatoes guy at home."

"To adventure and cajones!" Craig said, smiling as he toasted Steve.

Several margaritas later, their appetites sated with tacos that didn't disappoint—in fact they had two more orders—the two of them stumbled out of the restaurant into the midday sun in the parking lot of El Jefe's.

As they headed to the Red Shark, a young, scruffy looking guy sitting on the hood of a car said to Craig, "Hey Asshole. Can you spare a dollar?"

Craig stopped and took a long look at the obnoxious panhandler, who had a "posse" of two other "ne'er-do-wells" with him. Craig wondered how successful that unique approach at asking for money had been as he also sized up how much damage he could do if he knocked the punk off the car.

Sensing what was in Craig's head, Steve gathered him up and moved him along to the Red Shark.

Getting into the car, Craig fumed, "What a jerk!"

"We don't need any trouble, Bro," Steve said, adding sarcastically. "And certainly not a gunfight after lunch."

"Point well taken," Craig conceded. Chuckling, he said: "I guess we're going to have to update our dining apparel to include color-coordinated bullet-proof vests."

As they drove off, Craig said, "I know you suggested that 'open carry' makes people more civil by necessity. For me, knowing that you're carrying made me think seriously about throwing some punches, even though there were three of them."

"But that's the thing, Bro. You never know if they're also carrying. It makes one back off from any confrontation."

Leaning back and exhaling as he drove, Craig said, "Fair enough. Of course you're right."

After pausing in thought, Craig asked, "I was just wondering. Why didn't your caution about confrontations apply to the blue-haired girl at Knuckleheads Saloon?"

"I guess I didn't perceive her as a threat," Steve said.

"Was it because she was female?" Craig asked.

Hesitating, Steve finally replied, "Good question. I guess I just didn't think about it."

"Let me ask the question another way," Craig said. "Would you have poured a beer on the head of a guy if he had done the same thing?"

Thinking about it for a minute, Steve replied, "To be honest, I don't know."

Pressing on, Craig said, "That leads me to another question. If the person who was appointed to head your history department had been a black man rather than a woman, would you still feel aggrieved?"

"Yes," Steve replied defiantly. "My grievance is that white men are being discriminated against."

"What if a white woman had been appointed?"

"I don't see any difference," Steve said. "My objection isn't about race or gender per se. It's about affirmative action for special groups at the expense of white men."

"Okay," Craig asked. "What if it were a white man?"

"I'd be okay with that since it wouldn't be affirmative action," Steve said.

"And you would assume that such an appointment would therefore be on the merits based on credentials?" Craig posited.

"Yes," Steve answered. "Where are you going with this?"

"Did you ever consider that the African American woman appointed to head your department just might have superior credentials to yours?"

Taking in a deep, audible breath, Steve said, "I guess it's possible."

"That brings me back to our conversation a couple of days ago. Strip race, gender, and victimhood out of your calculations and focus on buffing your own credentials. Like Tammy, I have faith in you, Bro."

Pausing, Steve said, "Thanks Craig."

As the two of them drove on, they were surprised by Pahrump. Wineries, golf courses, casinos—without the buzz of Las Vegas, and, most surprisingly, a large lake framed not by a fake 'backdrop' of mountains like you might see on a movie set or a foreshortened photo but the real deal.

"Okay," Craig said. "The surprise is just ahead—the 'Chicken Ranch,' which sits on forty acres."

"What in the hell is the 'Chicken Ranch?'" Steve asked.

"It's a brothel, Bro."

"What? You mean a whorehouse?"

"It's legal and licensed. You can have your pick of 'courtesans.'"

"Are you shitting me?"

"We both wanted an 'immersive' experience. It can't get any more 'immersive' than this." Craig laughed. "You said you were becoming adventuresome. How about you pursuing Gonzo's quest for a 'back door beauty?'"

"No way, Bro. Not me," Steve said, recoiling in horror.

"Steve, this is one time where the phrase 'What happens in Las Vegas stays in Las Vegas' is true."

"No way, Craig. I'd bring it home with me."

"Bring what home with you? The 'courtesans' are tested regularly, and condoms are required. I'm confident that they even have some of the 'small' condoms you'd need," Craig teased. "No STDs would be traveling home with you. And wasn't it you who declared at Knuckleheads that 'what Tammy doesn't know won't hurt her?'"

Ignoring Craig's taunt, Steve replied plaintively, "I'd know. And knowing I had cheated on Tammy would be a stain that wouldn't wash away. If the tables were turned, I'd be devastated. Besides, aren't you the guy always bugging me about calling Tammy and urging me to claw my way back to the top of the mountain?"

"Okay, Lady Macbeth," Craig said teasingly. "It's just sex—another rush like so many others."

"That's why you've never gotten to the top of the mountain," Steve shot back. "You treat sex as a commodity—just another 'hit.' For me, it's so much more than that."

"Maybe." Craig said, laughing. "The place is called the 'Chicken Ranch' because of all the chicks inside—not for the 'chicken-shits' afraid to go in. Are you scared you won't be able to get it up? Hell, when you beat-off, do you only think of Tammy? How about Becky Thompson? Or Sophia Caputo?"

Flustered, Steve said, "I'll be honest, I have fantasized when beating-off, but as you've pointed out repeatedly, there's a difference between fantasy and reality."

"But which is more twisted?" Craig asked. "Don't you remember Duke musing about just that?"

As Steve shifted nervously in his seat, Craig finally said, "Okay, Bro. Suit yourself. I respect your decision. And your comment about sex being a commodity for me may be accurate. I'll have to think about it. Nevertheless, I'm going to get my hit. How about calling Tammy while you wait for me?"

Slumping dejectedly as if he were about to be swallowed whole by the vinyl upholstery, Steve finally said, "There's no one in this world that I respect and admire more than you, Craig. Please don't take my reluctance as a criticism of you. To each his own. I just can't."

"It's all cool, Steve. We're in different places in our lives. I'll be honest—your observation about my approach to sex, although it stings, may be right on. And I know you said it because you're all for me. For now, however, it's nice to know exactly how much this bit of entertainment will cost me—unlike my two marriages."

With that, Craig exited the Red Shark to score another 'high' among the many available in Las Vegas.

Steve tried to call Tammy while he waited, but there was no cellphone coverage.

***

The trip back to Las Vegas was uneventful. The easy bonhomie between the two of them remained.

"I think I can say this without fear of contradiction," Steve said. "'Legal' prostitution and 'bordellos' are one 'sin' that will remain in Las Vegas."

"Oh Steve, don't be so naïve. Prostitution is the world's oldest profession—even the Bible mentions it. Just like Prohibition didn't work, neither does the outlawing of prostitution. It exists everywhere—even in Columbia, Missouri. By making it legal and regulating it, sex workers are protected from brutal pimps and abusive 'Johns,' are checked regularly for STDs, and aren't forever stigmatized with criminal records if they seek other employment."

"Maybe so, but it will never be legalized outside Nevada. There's a difference between right and wrong and what society is prepared to sanction."

"Just like recreational marijuana would never be legalized in Missouri?" Craig countered. "We'll see. Maine just passed a law decriminalizing prostitution, and Massachusetts is considering doing the same. Canada and most of Europe have already done so. And if that doesn't blow your mind, Oregon just legalized 'psilocybin,' the hallucinogen in magic mushrooms—a move that was once unthinkable. As Hunter S. Thompson once said, 'Morality is temporary, wisdom is permanent.'"

Both of them were hot and dusty and took long showers after getting back to the Bellagio. Because they had reservations at L'Atelier at eight-thirty, dress that night was smart casual, even though they were going to spend time on Fremont Street before dinner. Each had a beer from the mini-bar with Steve lounging on the bed heckling Craig about taking some Doxycycline to treat his impending venereal disease. Craig perused one of his guidebooks while laughing and brushing off Steve's taunts.

They called the dispatcher and arranged for a car to pick them up at the front entrance at six p.m. They bumped into Tobey Maguire in the lobby.

"I've been rethinking the idea of using jet skis on the lagoon, Tobey," Craig said with a big smile. "For whatever reason, my desire has evaporated just like the twelve million gallons of water lost from the lagoon each year."

"I'm pleased," Tobey replied in a serious tone, ignoring the comment about evaporation. "We want to do everything we can to maximize your fun while visiting, but that was one thing I just couldn't pull off."

"Understood, Tobey. And I appreciate your effort. I just wanted you to know that it's no longer on my 'bucket list.'"

As Craig and Steve exited the Bellagio to catch their ride, the two of them laughed in two-part harmony while clutching each other arm-in-arm.

Driving once again through the dazzling seductions of casino after casino and other entertainment venues, they arrived at the "Fremont Street Experience" in downtown—the original "Strip." The pedestrian mall occupies the westernmost five blocks of Fremont Street, including the area known for years as "Glitter Gulch," and portions of adjacent streets.

"'Glitter Gulch' featured a long runway with three poles where 'skin' was always in fashion," Craig mentioned. "Most of that action, like the 'Chicken Ranch,' is on the outskirts of Las Vegas at this point."

"I'll ask again," Steve asked. "Does all this information come from your guidebooks or from firsthand experience?"

"Guidebooks, Bro. As we discussed, I find them invaluable when traveling."

The pedestrian mall is an open-air promenade of gaming, dining, and entertainment, including seventy restaurants, three stages with free live entertainment year-round, and the "Viva Vision Light Show." The cluster of casinos, including icons like the "Golden Gate," "Golden Nugget," and "Binion's," wooed passersby with AC gushing from wide-open doors, luring them inside out of the heat with the loosest slots in town and free drinks for those gambling. More than twenty-four million people visit Las Vegas each year, and the "Fremont Street Experience" is a magnet. Many make a point of touching Binion's "Million Dollar Wall" of cash for good luck; Craig and Steve were no exceptions.

The two of them were pulled into the more than a quarter-of-a-mile-long Viva Vision Light Show, almost powerless to resist—like celestial objects being sucked into a black hole. What for years has been the world's largest video screen is almost fourteen hundred feet long, ninety feet wide, and suspended ninety feet above the pedestrian mall with vivid 3D graphics and powerful surround sound. There are numerous multi-sensory, original vignettes like *Mothership,* which features action-packed space battles with celestial backgrounds. *Fluid Lucidity* delivers a series of mind-bending abstract visual spectacles. *Garden of Eden* displays alien jungles teeming with flora and fauna, unlike any nature show on TV. The light shows include live bands and DJs that combine art, music, and emotion in an immersive experience—without VR goggles—that alters one's perception. Multi-generational crowds participate in sing-alongs that transform Fremont Street into a street party unlike any other.

"My God," Steve gasped, "I feel like I'm in the eye of a storm with all my senses fully engaged. 'Sight' and 'hearing' are obvious—but also 'touch' with the vibrations triggering the firing of countless nerve endings. I'm not sure if the 'smell' and 'taste' sensations are produced by the show or by my body's reaction to so many stimuli—but they're also present."

Steadying himself against Craig as the crowd swept by in an endless stream, Steve continued, "All I can compare this to is an other-worldly tornado I once lived through back home—with roofs being blown off houses and cars being tossed like ragdolls with me observing it all in a bizarre pocket of tranquility—like an out-of-body experience. Strangely enough, what I remember most is the overwhelming smell of ozone—which reminded me of bleach. This 'Show' really has to be experienced first-hand. I'm not sure I could describe it to Tammy or the kids in a way that does it justice."

"It's not exactly like Duke's drug-induced vision of his dead grandmother crawling up his leg with a knife in her teeth," Craig said, "but equally surreal."

Each of the 'vignettes' takes around seven minutes and at least an hour watching the Viva Vision Light Show was recommended by Craig's Guidebooks. The two of them took their time taking it all in, swilling martinis, and letting the show transport them down the rabbit hole. [xxxii]

"Let's do the super-hero zipline," Craig suggested.

"What in the hell is that?" Steve asked.

"You'll see. Just come with me."

With that, the two of them ascended the eleven-story "Slotzilla," the world's largest slot machine featuring kitschy Las Vegas icons like giant dice and an enormous martini glass.

"My God, this is disorienting, Bro," Steve observed. "After a while, it's hard to distinguish what's real and what's fantasy. I feel like I passed through the 'looking glass' [xxxiii] waiting for chess pieces to talk to me—or I'm in the song by the Jefferson Airplane where Alice is ten feet tall." [xxxiv]

"Yeah." Craig said, laughing. "And all this alcohol is probably not helping."

Suspended prone in "Super-Hero mode" on the zipline, they launched, at thirty-five miles per hour, under the canopy of Viva Vision into the bowels of the Fremont Street Experience, finally being deposited in front of the Golden Gate Casino.

The two of them had hidden water bottles in their clothes and sprayed water on the crowds on Fremont Street as they rode the zip line, giggling like the drunken teenagers they once were spitting water on the inhabitants of the next jail cell when they were in protective custody in Columbia.

"Now that—was exhilarating," Steve enthused. "I felt like I was inside a pinball machine when we were on Fremont Street experiencing the Viva Vision Show. The ride under the canopy made me feel like I was the pinball."

"Wild, isn't it?" Craig marveled.

"Let's check out the Golden Gate," Craig said. "It's not a place you'd take your grandmother—or the elderly woman your family has embraced. The bikini-clad dancing dealers and the 'flair' bartenders at the OneBar are special attractions. I also want to get to the Golden Nugget and Binion's. As I mentioned earlier, the Guidebooks say that the slots and other games are looser on Fremont Street. More importantly, although money isn't an issue, it will feel like a win each time we get a free drink while gambling. It's like that 'all you can eat' buffet we used to frequent when we were in college. Sort of like gluttonous Augustus Gloop in *Charlie and the Chocolate Factory*."
xxxv

"I don't think the 'Woke Police' allow you to reference that book without 'trigger warnings' or eliminating offensive words like 'gluttonous.'" Steve said laughing.

Laughing as well, Craig replied, "I can only reference that image by memory because your crowd has probably burned the book."

Not rising to the bait—even though it was liberals who were attacking the book—Steve said, "Let's try some blackjack. I understand the odds of the House winning are only fifty-one percent."

"Yeah," Craig said. "Most casinos would prefer to eliminate blackjack altogether, but the customers insist on keeping it. The only reason the odds favor the House is because they go second, which allows them to win if a player 'busts' on his draw or, if no bust, it allows the House to react to the card or cards the player receives when asking for a 'hit.' The skill in the game is math: playing probabilities. The probability of the player winning increases as the number of decks of cards decreases. The older Fremont Street casinos use a smaller number of decks than, say, a Bellagio."

"How does a smaller number of decks help?" Steve asked. "Wouldn't you have to calculate the probability of which cards remain?"

"Exactly," Craig said. "It's called 'card counting.' See that table next to us? Watch this."

"Watch what?"

"Do you see that guy with the beard who keeps winning?" Craig asked.

"Yeah. What about him?" Steve replied.

"There's a pit boss watching him. He's the one with glasses, ear-phones, and stern look. They're easy to spot since they're the only ones not having fun. I suspect the bearded guy is counting cards."

"Didn't we just talk about keeping cards in mind to try and calculate probabilities?" Steve asked. "Is that illegal? It sounds like good technique."

"No—it's not illegal. However, this is a private casino, and the proprietors have the right to ask someone to leave. Let's face it, you or I might try counting cards, but we're amateurs."

Sure enough, the bearded man received a tap on the shoulder and was escorted out of the casino by the pit boss.

Craig and Steve jumped in enthusiastically and played Blackjack, Slots, Roulette, and other games as they roamed from one casino to another—quaffing free drinks with abandon.

"I'm feeling a little woozy, Craig," Steve said plaintively.

"Let's get some fresh air," Craig urged.

As they exited the casino along Fremont Street, they spotted a big Polynesian-looking guy in a Hawaiian shirt wearing a "lei."

Chuckling, Steve whispered to Craig, "My God. Could that be the real Gonzo?"

"Let's find out."

Openly admiring the lei, Craig said to the man, "That looks like the real deal with genuine Ti leaves and orchids rather than plastic."

"It is. I got it at the 'Cal' just around the corner. The hotel and casino caters to Native Hawaiians like me. Check it out."

With that, the two of them began walking over to the California Hotel & Casino, which has a large sign on the marquee: "Aloha Spoken Here."

As they began to walk, they were immediately accosted by "Spider-Man."

"Hey guys," Spidey said. "Want a picture with a superhero?"

"No thanks," Craig replied.

Batman leaped forward and screamed at Spidey, "This is my turf. Move on, or I'll move you."

Bumping chests confrontationally, Spidey challenged. "You and who else?"

As this dustup was taking place, Craig and Steve noticed other Marvel action figures approaching aggressively.

"Let's get out of here," Steve said.

As they walked on, another hustler approached.

"Interested in an escort service?" he asked.

Craig and Steve simply shook their heads "no" and kept moving.

"Hey guys. Want some 'Molly?'" asked another. "How about 'devils breath, tranqs?' You name it; I've got it."

The street was awash with hawkers pushing bracelets, trinkets, and other tchotchke.

Between dodging hustlers and the crowds of tourists, many of whom were tipsy, getting to the Cal was like salmon swimming upstream, navigating rapids while avoiding bears and anglers.

As they were pushed along and jostled by throngs of people, Craig advised Steve, "Put your wallet in your front pocket. I haven't seen one yet, but this scene is rife with potential for pickpockets."

Finally running the gauntlet, the two of them paused at the entrance of the Cal to get their bearings.

"I always wondered how people get crushed in stampedes at soccer games," Steve said. "We're both big guys but I felt like I was being swept up in a flood that I couldn't resist."

"Agreed," Craig replied. "Let's get a car from the Bellagio for the trip back to Fremont. I hate to say it, Steve, but I think that the flood you describe and our inability to resist is a perfect metaphor for what's happening to America."

Steve let Craig's comment drop without inquiry or other response.

After their exchange, they surveyed the gaming tables for their next move.

Approaching one of the Craps tables, Craig struck up a conversation with an observer, a Polynesian man who both the Woke and Anti-Woke could agree was the size of a Buick. "So what's with the sign advertising that the casino speaks 'Aloha?'"

"The Cal has a long tradition of arranging special travel deals and targeted marketing to Hawaiians. As you can see, the dealers all wear Hawaiian shirts, and snacks like 'Spam Musabi' and 'Poi' are featured."

"Sorry—what's that?" Steve asked.

Chuckling, the Hawaiian, who introduced himself as "Kahale," said, "'Spam Musabi' is rice and spam wrapped in seaweed. 'Poi' is a Hawaiian specialty made from the taro root. It's cooked, mashed with water and allowed to ferment. The degree of fermentation determines the taste."

"Is it like kimchi?" Steve asked.

His 'ample' body shaking like a roughly idling automobile, Kahale burst into laughter and said, "Poi is an acquired taste—a starch that kept many Hawaiians alive. The taro root was brought to Hawaii from their native islands centuries ago by voyagers of Polynesian origin. Although they're both fermented, it doesn't taste like kimchi, which uses cabbage as its base. Most 'Haoles' are not fans and would tell you it tastes like paste."

"I think I'll pass," Steve said.

Laughing, Craig said, "I guess your experimentation with exotic foods has its limits, Steve."

"Yeah," Steve replied. "It doesn't sound like it would mix too well with vodka."

"You may not know this," Kahale said, "but Las Vegas has the largest population of Native Hawaiians outside the Islands—around twenty-two thousand at this point. We call Las Vegas the 'Ninth Island.'"

"Why is that?" Craig asked.

"As heart wrenching as it is to leave paradise, most Native Hawaiians simply can't afford to live there anymore. Hawaii imports almost all of its food. which makes it outrageously expensive, and there are very strict building restrictions to preserve the natural beauty of the islands for rich people. Las Vegas has constant entertainment, a low cost of living, and we can actually own a house here."

Pausing, Kahale said, "The desert is our ocean. We cherish our traditions: teaching the Native Hawaiian language, blessing babies with a 'Ho'ola'a ceremony, celebrating traditional festivals, making leis for special occasions, and even practicing with outriggers on Lake Mead. It's a very tight-knit community."

"Fascinating," Craig said. "Do you grow the Ti plants here?"

"No. On the islands, they are readily accessible. We can't grow them here in the desert. We have Ti leaves and orchids shipped in from Hawaii or California."

"Thanks for sharing, Kahale. Yours is both a sad but happy story. Steve and I have enjoyed meeting and talking with you but have to split. Aloha."

"Aloha!" Kahale said to both of them with a generous smile and a bear hug for each.

Not wanting to fight through the throngs of hustlers and tourists, they called the Bellagio for a car. As they drove back to Fremont Street, Craig said, "Man— thinking about what Kahale said, I guess Joni Mitchell was half right. They're not paving paradise but are putting it in a 'tree museum.'"

"Yeah," Steve replied. "I admire their courage and adaptability—just like the original Polynesian explorers—particularly in light of my own trepidation about relocating from Columbia. I was struck by Kahale's comment about the desert being their ocean. Talk about altered reality."

In the Golden Nugget lobby, they were able to view the "Hand of Faith," the largest gold nugget in existence—the second biggest ever discovered—weighing sixty-one pounds, shaped like a hand.

"Okay, 'Answer Man,' why is it called 'Hand of Faith?'" Steve asked.

"You're the religious guy here, Steve. I thought you'd know," Craig said tauntingly.

"Not a clue."

"Your question was answered in one of my guidebooks," Craig revealed. "In addition to looking like a hand, the discoverer, a guy named Bep Hillier, had a dream of the nugget that was so vivid, he drew a picture of it, and had a neighbor sign the picture back in 1980. Twelve days later, using a metal detector, he found the nugget only six inches below the surface—the drawing having been a freakishly accurate depiction. Hillier and his family were down-and-out at the time, living in a converted bus in Australia, but his sale of the nugget to the casino made him an instant millionaire. Thus: 'The Hand of Faith.'"

All of a sudden, Steve reacted with alarm. "Oh my God. I hate to tell you this, Craig, but I just realized it's nine-fifteen. Our reservation at L'Atelier was at eight-thirty."

"Oh well. Screw it. Let's party on. We'll just grab snacks at the gaming tables."

The two of them ended up at one of the Craps tables at Binion's. Steve was full of an alcohol-fueled swagger that convinced him he could win.

He made 'Pass' bets and lost the first couple of rounds. He then became the shooter and won his first roll with a seven.

"I'm feeling it tonight," he announced confidently to Craig and the other players as he rolled again. When an eleven came up, Steve jumped in the air and yelled out, "Yes!"

He kept winning, and the players at the table cheered him on as many surfed the wave. Others from nearby tables soon began to congregate around the action and joined in the cheering. Craig couldn't help but notice that Steve began to emulate the "strutting" Paradise, simulated spiking a football with each winning roll, followed by an exaggerated "moonwalk." He was flying.

A one hundred dollar even money bet yielded one hundred dollars. Letting it ride, two hundred dollars then became four hundred, on and on until the original one hundred dollar bet totaled six thousand four hundred dollars.

"Take some of that money off the table, Steve. Sooner or later you'll roll Craps," Craig implored.

"Nah. I'm feeling lucky tonight," Steve said as he let his winnings ride. "I've always tried to imagine what it was like to hit the winning shot in basketball. You've had that feeling. I never had it until now. It's exhilarating."

Eventually, the inevitable happened, and he lost the entire pot.

"I still feel lucky. I'm going to keep playing until I win it all back even if I have to borrow."

With that, Craig hustled him away from the Craps table. "Never play to 'win it back.' And never borrow to play. I think you have a problem."

"I don't have a problem. I'm just having fun," Steve protested. "Just like you said, winning at Craps is like having sex or taking a hit of 'Molly.'"

"'Molly?' You haven't done that since college. I thought we were going to abstain on this trip, Steve."

"We are," Steve said. "But man, winning is such a high."

"Like drugs, it's also addictive. Stay away from the casinos in Missouri, Bro. And definitely stay away from online sports betting when it comes to town. They imitate many of the addictive inducements of slots, like small rewards, to keep you playing. Hell, you freaked out about the Chicken Ranch. At least you can know the cost there. Betting can be a bottomless pit. Let's get out of here and take a fling on the 'High Roller.'"

After summoning a car from the Bellagio, the two of them decamped for the Caesar's Entertainment attraction. At five hundred-fifty feet, it held the title as the world's largest Ferris Wheel until 2021, when it was eclipsed by the 'Ain Dubai,' which stands at eight hundred-twenty feet, in that other desert fantasy land—packed with over-the-top theme parks and numerous attractions, but no gambling because of Islamic laws. The High Roller has twenty-eight transparent pods holding up to forty passengers each. There are sweeping three hundred sixty-degree views of the glittering lights of Las Vegas, with each revolution taking thirty to forty minutes. Craig picked up tickets for several rides. The iconic attraction features two thousand lights choreographed to music. While there's no opportunity to sophomorically spray water or a shaken carbonated beverage on bystanders like there would be on an open Ferris Wheel at a county fair, the enclosed 'Happy Half Hour' cabins include an open bar with free drinks as part of the price of a ticket. Craig and Steve swilled martinis, and belted out 'Viva Las Vegas,' along with others in the pod, at the prompting of an 'Elvis' impersonator.

Stumbling back to the Bellagio, holding on to each other for balance while laughing non-stop as if everything was funny, the two of them passed the Patisserie Chocolate Fountain—the largest in the world. The shop was closed, but they were able to observe the twenty-seven foot fountain featuring three rivers of dark, two of milk, and one of white chocolate cascading down through a maze of twenty-five suspended glass vessels, creating a mosaic effect and refracted light on the sculptured glass chandelier.

"Augustus Gloop would be in heaven," Steve declared. "And after he spent some time here, even the 'Woke' crowd would be hard pressed to avoid use of the word 'fat.'"

"Let's put the culture wars—and us—to bed," Craig said.

Back in their room, Steve retrieved a couple of beers from the minibar.

Taking a sip of beer, Craig said, "You don't talk much about your kids, Steve. Tell me about them."

"I think you know that George is fourteen and Jennifer twelve. There's not much to tell; they're just regular kids," Steve said.

"Do you have photos?"

"Of course," Steve said as he grabbed his iPhone. "Let me show you."

Studying the photos closely, Craig observed, "They're both good looking kids.'" Laughing, he added, "Fortunately, they both look like their mother."

Laughing as well, Steve said, "Thanks, Pal. I know you're just trying to needle me, but I think you're right. George inherited my 'tall' genes but no athletic ability or real interest in sports. He's a straight 'A' student and, like his mother, an avid reader."

"I think that's terrific, Steve. How much do either of us use our athletic ability at this point?"

"True. My father attended all my sporting events and cheered me on. He was proud of me. It was something we shared. I think he was also living a bit vicariously since he was not an athlete himself."

"So maybe George will be the next Bill Gates or Jeff Bezos. Isn't the goal to give a child a foundation to become whatever he or she is destined to be?"

"Yeah. Although I have to admit it would be fun to cheer George on in some sport."

"Tammy mentioned that the kids were at swimming lessons when I stopped by. That's a sport," Craig offered.

"It can be. But neither George nor Jennifer are on a swim team. They get swimming lessons at our insistence—so they're safe around water and to get some exercise."

"That's good parenting, Bro. Have you tried something you can do together like golf or fishing?"

"No. I'm not very good at golf. I do enjoy fishing from time to time, but George hasn't shown much interest."

"I remember seeing a cartoon with two fat—whoops, I guess I have to say 'very big'—guys on a golf cart with one saying to the other, 'We golf; therefore we're athletes,'" Craig said, laughing. "It doesn't matter how good you are. It's spending time with each other."

"When did you become a 'parenting guru?" Steve asked sarcastically.

"Oh, I have plenty of experience from the other side of the equation," Craig said, grimacing. "And how about Jennifer?"

"She's a sweet child, although she's become moody and withdrawn lately. I suspect it's related to the onset of puberty," Steve said.

"Maybe," Craig noted. "As we've discussed, however, I'd check on her social media use."

"Hmmm! I think that's a good suggestion. I must admit, I hadn't given it much thought."

"So besides being sweet and somewhat moody, what's Jennifer like?" Craig asked.

"She's also a reader, and quite frankly, pretty athletic. She can lap George in swimming."

"How about organized team sports?" Craig asked. "With Title IX, we've seen the emergence of American women as world-class athletes dominating in sports like soccer and basketball internationally."

"Jennifer has shown some interest in cheerleading," Steve said.

"That's great. But have you encouraged her to try basketball, for example? You could actually give her some valuable pointers." Craig said.

"Not really. I would support her—but I can't say I've encouraged her."

"You may not realize it, but the rise of American women in sports is often nurtured by enthusiasm from fathers."

"I guess I hadn't considered it," Steve said. "But if Jennifer did take to sports and I got involved, that would leave George on the outside looking in."

"You'd have to work at other activities you can do together. I mentioned golf. How about chess, or antique cars, or other things that might pique his interest? If he hasn't already seen it, you might introduce him to the 'Dreams of O' VR video or do some video games—so long as it's structured and limited—all things in moderation. In fact, you might consider bringing the whole family to Las Vegas to try the actual 'O' Show, or gaming at the Circus-Circus Arcade, or any of a number of family appropriate entertainment venues."

"I haven't given it much thought," Steve said. "Shame on me. I think those are good suggestions, although we certainly couldn't afford to stay at the Bellagio."

"There are plenty of less expensive, family-oriented hotels," Craig responded. "Shifting gears, maybe you could rent an RV and travel to Bryce Canyon, or just have father/son and father/daughter outings for pizza and a movie."

"I appreciate your thoughts, Bro."

"I hope I'm not being too personal, Steve, but doing the math tells me that George didn't come along until you were thirty-three or so. Was that intentional? You mentioned earlier that you simply followed in your father's footsteps. I suspect he didn't wait to have kids until that age."

"No, it wasn't intentional. Tammy and I struggled conceiving, and once we did, she had a miscarriage. We were devastated and came to believe that maybe children weren't in the cards. When George came along, it was like a miracle."

"All babies are miracles, Steve."

"Amen." Steve sighed. "George's birth was the happiest day of my life. It's also why, fourteen years later, I despair at our lack of connection."

"At the risk of sounding like a broken record, you have to work at it. What any child wants, no matter how old, is time alone with each of their parents."

Pausing, Steve asked, "Craig, you mentioned that you have plenty of experience on parenting from the child's side of the equation. What did you mean by that?"

Hesitating at first, Craig finally said, "My parents, God rest their souls, were good people. But they didn't have a clue about parenting and were very 'transactional' about the parenting 'thing.' My sister Olivia and I had a nanny when we were young. We were sent to boarding schools when we were older. My parents were very matter-of-fact about it. They always rationalized that the boarding schools would do a better job of raising us than they would. Knowing who they were and what they valued, I suspect they were right."

"Some would see boarding schools as an unbelievable privilege and opportunity," Steve said. "I must admit that I couldn't bear to send my kids off even if I had the money, but the prep schools do expand worldviews, develop networks, and create a fantastic platform to do whatever you want."

"I think that's true. But read some of John Irving's novels mentioning the boarding school experience. It can be extremely lonely, austere, and even traumatic while at the same time being a training ground for seeing the world as it is and growing up quickly."

"But you must have spent summers and holidays with your parents," Steve said.

"We were packed off to summer camp every year, which once again, was a mixed bag. Swimming, fishing, baseball, goofing around with peers—how can you beat that? But both Olivia and I always felt something was missing. It wasn't 'homesickness' per se, because there wasn't the sweet pull of home in the traditional sense. Still, there was a hollow feeling that ate at us—particularly as our peers talked fondly of 'home' and we tried to glean what that meant to them—it was clearly more than simply a place to hang your hat. As to holidays, they were fairly formal affairs carefully dovetailed into my parents' busy social and charitable schedules. You marveled earlier about my mother talking to me about sex. They always talked to us like we were simply small adults."

"Craig, I'm still sorry about your loss of Olivia. I only met her once, when she came to Mizzou for Homecoming Weekend. She was delightful. I know Olivia was a couple of years older than you, but it was still shocking to realize that someone roughly our age—an age when we believed we were invincible—could die from cancer."

"Thanks, Bro. It was hard to accept and still is. Olivia was my real family. We had a shared childhood, and she was my 'Big Sister' in every sense of the word—always there for me. My parents broke up shortly after she died and, of course, both of them are now gone. I miss her terribly."

"You would have been a great parent, Craig—and still can be," Steve said.

"Maybe, maybe not," Craig replied wistfully. "I am my parents' child."

"Let's get some sleep," Craig said as he pitched his beer bottle into the trash can."

"I'm all in," Steve replied as he tossed his empty at the trash can but missed, the bottle shattering into many pieces.

"Still shooting bricks," Craig laughed as he brushed up the shards with the covers of a couple of magazines.

Laughing as well, Steve said, "See you at noon."

Chapter 7
What Happens in Las Vegas, Leaves Las Vegas

"Man—I think my head is going to explode," Steve moaned. "What time is it anyway?"

"It's almost noon, Steve. I've been up reading for a couple of hours but decided to let you finally sleep in. Want some 'hair of the dog' from the minibar?"

"Just to prove I know the Bible," Steve replied, "Proverbs 26:11 warns: 'As a dog returneth to his vomit, a fool repeats his folly.' As you probably know, the 'hair of the dog' remedy—if it works at all—simply delays the inevitable reckoning."

"So—do you want a beer?"

"Oh, what the hell?" Steve said. "Did you get any Doxy yet? You can wash it down with your beer."

Ha! Ha! Ha! Craig replied. "No worries, Bro. The alcohol will kill any STDs, which is why I'm determined to drink as much as possible."

Opening a couple of beers and sharing one with Steve, Craig said, "I've got a late lunch reservation at the Top of the World Restaurant at the 'Strat.' It's not L'Atelier but is supposed to have great steaks and the Wine Spectator Award of Excellence for twenty-four years in a row. More importantly, the restaurant is on the one hundred sixth floor and revolves three hundred sixty degrees every eighty minutes, providing spectacular views of the Las Vegas valley and mountains undisturbed by the glitter of lights we would encounter at dinner."

"Sounds good," Steve said. "As I've mentioned, I'm a meat and potatoes guy, and what sounds a little closer to home cooking—at least for me—will hit the spot."

"Just a heads-up but I have some 'entertainment' planned before lunch," Craig advised.

"Okay. I guess I'm game for anything," Steve said.

The two of them showered, dressed, and headed over to the Strat.

The Strat's 'SkyPod' is the tallest freestanding observation tower in the United States, rising to one thousand, one hundred forty-nine feet. The tower looks like a space needle with a twelve-story bubble on top. You can access the two level indoor and outdoor observation deck on the one hundred eighth floor.

Before going to the restaurant, at Craig's urging, the two of them strapped into the so-called "X-Scream," which is advertised as a roller coaster ride "like no other." Craig slipped the operator a couple of twenties so that he and Steve got the front seats. The ride sits on what looks like a giant teeter-totter that suddenly tilts one end at a steep angle so that the riders plunge down headfirst over the edge of the building—ultimately extending out twenty-seven feet. There, they are left to dangle weightlessly eight hundred sixty-six feet above the ground before the teeter totter rights itself, pulling the riders up from the brink, and then tips downward, propelling the riders out over the edge once again.

"Holy shit, Craig," Steve said, his face flushed and his heart pounding. "That was terrifying. I was convinced that something had gone wrong and we were goners. Going back to an earlier comment, I'm not sure what's more twisted: fantasy or reality."

"Don't be a pussy, Bro. The ride wasn't as scary as the 'Chicken Ranch,' was it?"

"Very funny. You're lucky I didn't upchuck all over you."

"That's why I wanted to do it before lunch," Craig teased. "Let's try the 'Big Shot.' It shoots riders up one hundred sixty feet at breathtaking speeds, launching from the nine hundred twenty-one foot platform up to the tower's mast at one thousand eighty-one feet and then down again. Before you can catch your breath, you're catapulted up again. The shot up is like a rocket with four G's of force."

"No thanks, Dude. Call me a 'pussy' if you want, but there's no way I'm getting on that thing. I'm feeling queasy and a little unsteady with my balance. In fact, I'm a little worried about the revolving restaurant and how unsettling that may be."

"Okay, Bro." Craig chuckled while putting his arm around Steve's back. "Let's go get a steak."

Stopping in mid-stride, Steve said, "Damn. I just realized I lost my ballcap during that ride. I don't know if it was the wind or the sudden jolt at the end."

Laughing, Craig said, "Bullshit. You probably lost the ballcap because you reached up to cover your eyes and knocked it off."

"Very funny, Dude."

"No worries. We can probably find it when we exit the SkyPod because no one will want a Royals hat."

Ha. Ha. Ha, Steve retorted.

Arriving at the restaurant, Craig suggested, "How about some wine?"

"I need something stiffer than that," Steve said.

Their waitress was a young woman named Alyssa. She made an immediate impression as an All-American girl with dirty blonde hair, a sturdy frame, and a welcoming persona. Smiling, she asked, "Can I start you with a drink?"

"I thought you'd never ask," Steve answered jokingly. "I'll have an Irish pour of Jameson—neat."

"What's an 'Irish pour?'" Alyssa asked.

"Have you heard of the 'Big Shot' Alyssa?" Steve asked.

"Do you mean the rocket ride here at the Sky Pod?"

Grinning, Steve said, "Similar—an 'Irish Pour' is over-the-top like the Big Shot. It's a double shot. Make it a triple."

"I'll have a bottle of the Medlock Ames Cabernet," Craig said. "I don't recall ever seeing it on a menu. I'm pleasantly surprised."

"I'll get those right away," Alyssa said cheerfully as she presented menus. As she turned to retrieve their drink orders, Steve abruptly stopped her.

"Before you leave, Alyssa, I have a request for you. Would you join me in an emphatic 'clap' on the count of three for my friend, Craig?"

Looking perplexed, Alyssa replied, good-naturedly, "Sure."

At the count of three, Steve and Alyssa harmonized a clap loud enough that it startled a couple dining nearby, resulting in a dropped fork clattering on a plate.

Laughing with abandon, Steve thanked Alyssa as she departed, still wearing a puzzled look on her face, while apologizing to the unnerved couple.

"Very funny," Craig said, "but I don't have 'The Clap.'"

Chuckling, Steve said, "I don't know, Bro. Gonnorrhea is making a big comeback nowadays. I keep telling you that a dose of Doxy will eliminate any doubts."

"And I keep telling you that the alcohol will take care of it—or transform me into blissful ignorance," Craig said joining in the laughter.

Changing the subject, Craig reminisced, "I mentioned visiting Redwoods National Park during a business trip. Afterwards, our hosts treated us to a delightful dinner at the Medlock Ames Winery at their Bell Mountain Ranch in the Alexander Valley of Sonoma County. The seating was at a long communal table outside in the Vineyard with beautiful weather and no bugs. It was one of the most romantic scenes I've ever been part of—unfortunately without, at least in my case, a romantic interest to share the magic—thereby making it incomplete. I remember the wines as being sublime, but it will be interesting to tease out if it truly was the wines or the 'gestalt' of the evening that made them so memorable."

"Sounds heavenly. I'm not ashamed to say once again that I envy you," Steve said. "I would love to walk in your shoes."

"Maybe—maybe not," Craig replied wistfully. "I hate to say it, but you sound a lot like those teenage girls who get depressed watching their peers portray an impossibly-perfect life on social media. Don't believe everything you see or hear."

Alyssa returned with their drinks.

Steve took a long slug of his whiskey, draining half of the glass. "My own version of 'Mother's Little Helper' after that 'X-Scream," he declared while grinning. [xxxvi]

"Have you had a chance to look at your menus?" Alyssa asked. "No rush."

"I know what I want," Steve declared emphatically. "I'd like the twenty-two ounce ribeye—medium rare."

Smiling, Craig said, "'Medium rare?' Good for you, Bro. I'll have the same."

"How about sides?" Alyssa asked.

"I'd like a baked potato with all the fixings," Steve replied. "And some Mac & Cheese."

"You're going full Mizzou on me, Steve. No vegetables? Okay, I'm all in with the same."

Snickering, Steve said, "What? Are you telling me Mac & Cheese doesn't qualify as vegetables?"

As Alyssa left to place their orders, Craig sipped his Cab.

"What's the verdict?" Steve asked.

"Excellent," Craig replied. "Both wine and cigar sommeliers talk a lot about the 'terroir,' and how the soil, topography, and climate influence the final product. There's no way to replicate the entire 'terroir' of that magical evening with this wine, but it goes a long way to getting there."

Scanning the horizon, Craig said, "Look at these views."

"Pretty spectacular," Steve enthused. "Do you see what looks like a lush mountain there on the south side of the Strip a couple of miles from here? Do you know what that is?"

"I think it's the mountain at Wynn Las Vegas," Craig replied. "It cost millions to build and features the three acre 'Lake of Dreams,' with its forty-foot waterfall and pine tree-topped surroundings. Apparently, there's a spiral staircase that takes you up through the treeline for a fantastic view. The lake comes alive at night with over four thousand brightly colored lights as well as holographic images, accompanied by music. My guidebooks tell me that dining by the lake is divine."

"Unbelievable," Steve said. "Yet another example of altered reality."

"You ain't seen nothing yet, Bro," Craig said. "Do you see that huge orb down by the Venetian?"

"Yeah. What in the hell is it?" Steve asked.

"It's the new 'Sphere.' It doesn't officially open until late September. I'm bummed that we didn't get to see the July 4th preview. It's something like three hundred sixty-six feet tall and over five hundred feet wide. It cost more than two billion dollars and is now the world's largest video screen, eclipsing even the Viva Vision Show. The screen is capable of over two hundred fifty million colors. Let me pull up some YouTube videos."

Looking at several of the videos, Steve said, "Oh my God. Can you imagine driving a car close by and looking up and seeing that giant, ominous eyeball looking down at you? And now it's a snow globe. And a jack-o'-lantern. And a black hole. This shot looks like waves undulating all over the sphere. Are those lava flows? It's also three dimensional—look at the figure seemingly inside the globe. Unreal!"

"They claim it's four dimensional," Craig said.

"I don't even know what that means," Steve replied.

"Tammy would tell you that God made man in three dimensions—height, length, and width—but that He himself is in the fourth dimension. As I understand it, the creators of the Sphere say that the fourth dimension—meaning 'time' in this instance—is also in play. Frankly, I'm a little unclear how that works. I do know that there are apparently something like one hundred sixty thousand speakers and vibrating seats that will take the concept of immersion for those attending a live music or sporting event at the Sphere to a different level."

"That's mind-boggling," Steve said.

"Agreed," Craig replied.

Leaning back and savoring a sip of wine, Craig continued, "As a historian, you might be interested in some historical notes about the Las Vegas valley. I was rereading and trying to memorize some of those facts as you slept this morning."

"Will there be a test at the end of your lecture, Professor Wells?" Steve teased.

"No test, but I think you'll find this informative. It provides context. The City of Las Vegas was founded in 1905 by a group of developers seeking to take advantage of artesian springs in the area to create a railroad stop between Salt Lake City and Los Angeles."

"I keep hearing about artesian springs but haven't seen any," Steve observed.

"I think it's like Pahrump with the springs once supporting alfalfa and cotton farms," Craig said. "No more now that the surface aquifers have been used up."

"The need for water," Craig noted, "led to the construction of the Hoover Dam between 1931 and 1936 during the Great Depression. The project brought thousands of workers to the area. Because the workers were mostly male—gambling, prostitution, and heavy drinking were prevalent—really just a continuation of the old mining days but with a lot more men. Nevada had outlawed gambling in 1909, and of course, the 18th Amendment introduced Prohibition in 1919. Some locals reportedly expressed surprise to hear that the 21st Amendment repealed Prohibition in 1933, claiming that they never knew drinking had been outlawed in the first place and never stopped, reflecting the ingrained 'Wild West' mentality."

"I just assumed that gambling was always legal in Nevada," Steve said.

"Just like the locals were unaware of Prohibition—or ignored it—I suspect they also ignored the laws against gambling. In any event, in 1931 Nevada repealed the ban on gambling. It was about that time that the mob infiltrated Las Vegas, fostering a variety of shady businesses. The state relaxed marriage and divorce laws, with 'quickie' divorces becoming a magnet. There are now three hundred marriages a day in Las Vegas. Think about it. That's around one hundred ten thousand marriages a year."

"Amazing," Steve said. "I wonder how many are officiated by Elvis impersonators."

"God only knows," Craig responded.

Craig continued, "Prostitution was outlawed federally by the ironically named 'Mann Act' in 1910, prohibiting the 'interstate' transportation of women for 'immoral' purposes. Prostitution has existed in Nevada forever, but 'in-state' prostitution was officially licensed in 1971, requiring public health checks—the same year as Hunter S. Thompson's book—but only in ten of Nevada's sixteen counties."

"And thus—between gambling and prostitution—the legend of 'Sin City' was born," Steve said, taking a sip of his drink.

"Exactly," Craig said. "The first casino opened in 1931. In 1920, the population of the Las Vegas Valley was a little over eight thousand people. Twenty years later, in 1940, the population was around sixteen thousand. In 1950, the year Senator Estes Kefauver was conducting a five-month probe of organized crime in Las Vegas, the

Valley had reached almost fifty thousand. Do you know what it is today?"

"I have no clue," Steve said.

"Just under three million. By 1955, there were ten casinos in Las Vegas. Can you guess how many there are now?"

"Again, I wouldn't even venture a guess."

"One hundred fifty. Liberace was the first big act in Vegas, starting in 1955, making what at the time was a shocking fifty thousand dollars a week. Elvis Presley started performing in town in 1956. The 'Rat Pack'—Frank Sinatra, Dean Martin, Sammy Davis, Joey Bishop, and Peter Lawford—performed for the first time in 1960, with the five of them appearing in the original *Ocean's Eleven* movie that same year. The film *Viva Las Vegas*, starring Elvis Presley and Ann Margret, was released in 1964. Other acts followed, including Wayne Newton, Evel Knievel, and Siegfried & Roy. The Beatles performed at the Convention Center in 1964. The legendary Howard Hughes arrived in Las Vegas in 1966 and proceeded to buy the Desert Inn and other hotels, ultimately leaving in 1970 after becoming Nevada's largest employer, casino owner, and property owner. In 1971, of course, *Fear and Loathing in Las Vegas* was published as a two-part story in *Rolling Stone*."

Alyssa appeared with their 'cowboy-sized' steaks and sides. "Enjoy, gentlemen. Is there anything else I can get you?"

"Yes, Alyssa, I'd like another Jameson," Steve said.

"Irish Pour?"

"Is there any other way?" Steve asked, chuckling.

"I'm good," Craig said, also laughing. "One bottle will do me for lunch. By the way, Alyssa, by any chance were you able to see the preview of the 'Sphere' on July 4th?"

"No. I was home at a cookout. One of my younger brothers sent me a link. I was freaked out by that giant eye. I'm not sure I want to be near it in a car or walking," she said with a visible shudder.

"Where are you from, Alyssa?" Craig asked. "I get the impression that no one is actually from Las Vegas, even though three million people live here now."

"I'm from a small town in North Dakota."

"So how did your brother know about the preview of the Sphere and send you a link?" Steve asked. In his astonishment, his face contorted to form what looked like a large question mark.

"My family may live in a rural community, but it's not on the dark side of the moon." Alyssa laughed. "The internet has made the world accessible to pretty much everyone."

"So what brought you here?" Craig asked.

"Our farm and the nearby small town are great, but I wanted to experience some of the glitter and glamour associated with Las Vegas. Plus, there are all kinds of jobs."

"Quite a contrast from rural North Dakota," Craig said.

"You think?" Alsyssa asked, snickering. "My parents weren't happy about me moving here, but I know they're just worried about me. My two younger brothers are excited and can't wait to visit."

"Have you found what you were looking for, Alyssa?" Craig asked.

"I guess so. At first it was thrilling if a bit disorienting, but after a while you get used to anything—although that giant eye will test me," she said with a grin—or was it a grimace? "I have to admit, it's only been a year and half but I'm feeling a little homesick. 'Glitter' in one person's eye is 'light pollution' in another's. As for jobs, heck, I can waitress anywhere."

Patrons of one of the nearby tables beckoned, and Alyssa excused herself to attend to them.

Taking a bite of his steak, Steve said, "Delicious. And you were right. Medium rare has much more flavor than well-done."

"Thanks, Steve. That's a big concession on your part. As was trying pulpo and oysters. I guess your newly adventurous nature has limits, however—no Poi."

"I don't even want to think about raw oysters or Poi—particularly with my upset stomach. Uggh! I was afraid that the revolving restaurant would keep my inners churning after the X-Scream, but it's actually kind of soothing—as long as I don't think about oysters," Steve said laughing.

"It's the whiskey doing the soothing—not the revolving restaurant. Thank God for any number of versions of 'Mother's Little Helper.' What pill do you think Duke would have popped?"

"God knows," Steve replied. "But I doubt it would have been only one."

Leaning back in his chair and taking a sip of his wine, Craig said, "The point of my limited stroll through history is to put in stark relief the Las Vegas Hunter S. Thompson encountered and what we're experiencing fifty years later. Las Vegas Valley had only two hundred fifty-five thousand people then—less than ten percent of what it has now. There were only a fraction of the casinos. The luxury resorts like the Bellagio, Venetian, Luxor, and others didn't exist. Attractions like the Viva Vision Light Show, the Luxor Light, the Bellagio Fountains, the Mirage Volcano, and now the Sphere had not been created. Yes, Circus Circus had trapeze artists flying over the gaming tables, but it irritated the gamblers, ultimately forcing the resort to transform itself with a Midway, Arcade and other entertainment separate from the casino."

"But the Red Shark is eternal," Steve said, laughing. "As are the Craps tables—and other excesses expressed in new and different ways."

"Indeed," Craig said. "In fact, I suspect 'Knock-Knock's' doppelganger was here back then. My point is that the days of the Rat Pack were the golden age for Las Vegas because it was so glamorous, exotic, and different from the rest of America—'Sin City.' In the minds of most, it might as well have been Kathmandu or Marrakesh. Trying to retain its reputation for being exotic and avant-garde, Las Vegas has been on the cutting edge of altered reality and immersive experiences, but just like the live entertainment, gambling, and other vices that made it distinctive, all of that is becoming mainstream in America with an eager audience thirsting for constant entertainment and distraction from every-day life—fantasy vs. reality."

"I hope I won't be around to see that happen," Steve said while draining his Jameson.

"But that's the point. It's already happening. Didn't you hear what Alyssa said? I was quite impressed with her take on the scene at such a young age. God help her younger brothers. At this point, I think there's a consensus that social media and other dopamine 'hits' are making us addicts craving instant and constant gratification. When you add to that toxic stew the isolation caused by the pandemic and social media, the gaslighting from constant misinformation, as well as the constant drip, drip of stress hormones associated with fear of you or a loved one becoming a victim of yet another mass shooting, there has been a huge increase in mental health issues. I've not seen any studies on this, but I think the same is true of ADHD. There's no question that the incidence has spiked. Is it biological or environmental? I think it's both—with one reinforcing the other."

Finishing their lunch, Steve laughed and said, "Buying into your thesis that we have a need for constant gratification, I'd like to see King Tut's tomb. It's the one hundredth anniversary since it was discovered."

"Let's do it," Craig replied.

***

Touring the King Tut Tomb at the Luxor is a very seductive experience. One follows in the shoes of famed archeologist Howard Carter as he unlocked the secrets of Tutankhamun's tomb. Starting with the antechamber, finding the burial chamber that houses the shrines, sarcophagus, and nested coffins that protected King Tut's mummy, and then coming face-to-face with the mummy itself and Tut's iconic "death mask," is surreal. The ton and half of gold in the actual tomb reflects the ancient Egyptian belief that gold was the "flesh" of the sun God Ra. The innermost coffin is mummy-shaped and made of solid gold, as is the iconic mask of the "boy king." At the Luxor, the replica gold looks authentic.

The tomb is brought to life through virtual reality and multimedia installations that transport you back in time, immersed in the sights and sounds of Carter's discovery. One can explore the different chambers and even virtually "grab" and inspect thousands of individual artifacts.

As they emerged from the exhibit, Craig and Steve struck up a conversation with an older woman from Philadelphia named Jean. She rhapsodized about the experience, saying it was superior to touring the actual tomb in Egypt, which she had done recently with a tour group sponsored by the University of Pennsylvania.

As they parted ways with Jean, Craig said in an aside to Steve, "Interesting observation by Jean. In addition to Italy and Egypt, as we've discussed, you can visit other cities and countries without leaving Las Vegas."

"You mentioned Paris and New York as two of those places," Steve said. "I haven't seen either here."

"Among other features, Paris Las Vegas, which is owned by Caesar's Entertainment, has half-scale replicas of the Eiffel Tower, as well as the Arc de Triomphe and La Fontaine des Mers," Craig said. "The front of the hotel suggests the Louvre, Musé d' Orsay, and the Paris Opera House. In fact, one of the best ways to see the Bellagio Fountain Show is from the faux Eiffel Tower."

"Now that you mention it, I've actually seen the replica Eiffel Tower from our hotel," Steve said.

"I understand that the New York New York Hotel-Casino is a one-third-sized replica of iconic Manhattan landmarks that includes the Empire State Building, Chrysler Building, Brooklyn Bridge, Statue of Liberty, fake tugboats spraying water in the 'harbor,' and other highlights," Craig said. "The towers are crammed with hotel rooms, and a steep roller coaster twists its way among them. Cemented into the wall in front of the Statue of Liberty are thirty glass display cases, each containing artifacts from '9/11.' It was only a coincidence that the World Trade Towers were not included when the fake skyline was built in 1996."

"Unbelievable," Steve marveled.

"It really is," Craig said. "I've been reading about Las Vegas pushing the boundaries of immersive art—combining art, technology, and theatricality. One example is *Arcadia Earth*, which is reputedly the first augmented reality journey through Earth. It includes art installations, projections, mapping, scent technology, and even robots. Another is *Particle Ink*, which is billed as a mind-bending, mixed reality installation that transports you through a portal into a different dimension where the virtual world blends with the physical world—taking you to a state between waking and sleeping. *Perception* is an immersive, digital art scene that eases you into the mind of Leonardo da Vinci in Renaissance Italy, where the 'Mona Lisa' and 'Last Supper' come alive in a quintessentially Vegas way."

Craig continued, "You may have heard of *Immersive Van Gogh*. It takes you inside Van Gogh's most iconic paintings as they come to life. Immersive apps can transform vibrant colors in the paintings, and you can even communicate with the artist through an AI tool. *Illuminarium* immerses you in a celestial experience that includes walking on the moon, weaving through an asteroid belt, and flying through a nebula. There are many more of these cutting-edge experiences. Do you have any interest?"

"My head is spinning, Bro. At least I've heard of *Immersive Van Gogh*."

"You've heard of it because, just like other altered reality offerings from Las Vegas, they ultimately leach into all of American life. *Immersive Van Gogh* opened in Las Vegas in 2021 but is already touring two dozen cities—but probably not Columbia, Missouri yet. As I mentioned before, the old saying about 'What happens in Las Vegas, stays in Las Vegas' has been turned on its head. It's now: 'What happens in Las Vegas will ultimately happen all over America.' Do you want to try the Van Gogh show?"

"I can probably see it near home," Steve said. "Tammy will be aghast that we haven't even visited the world-class Bellagio Gallery of Fine Art."

"I don't know if the Bellagio Gallery has any examples of 'pentimentos,'" Craig mused, "but it would be so Las Vegas."

"What's a 'pentimento?'" Steve asked.

"The word comes from the Italian word 'pentirsi' which means to repent or change one's mind. It's where one painting covers another on a canvas. Only by removing the subsequent layer of paint can one see the original painting. And how does one know how many paintings are covered over—like Russian nesting dolls? It's a perfect metaphor for things not being what they seem, representing, at least for me, the distortions and illusions everywhere in our lives nowadays."

"How in the hell do you know that? Surely that isn't in your guidebooks," Steve complained.

"No, it isn't in the guidebooks. Have you forgotten that my second wife ran an art gallery? Not only did she acquaint me with the term—she was the human embodiment of a pentimento—it just took me some time to scrape off the outer layer of paint."

"That's too deep for me, Bro," Steve said. "Let's check out the *Illuminarium* space voyage."

"Sound good," Craig replied.

The two of them went 'all-in' pretending to be Captain Kirk and Mr. Spock on the starship 'Enterprise' navigating the cosmos while sipping vodka from 'nips' they had stashed in their pockets.

Emerging from the 'space voyage,' Steve gasped, almost out of breath, "That was surreal. Again, Duke was right. You don't need drugs to have a hallucinogenic 'trip' here in Las Vegas. In fact, the various immersive experiences have been overwhelming."

Pausing as he focused his thoughts, Steve said, "I must admit, at this point I'm reminded of an experience I had my first year in Little League baseball. At the end of the season, the League had a celebratory picnic for all of the players with, among other things, all-you-can-eat watermelon. You know how competitive and stupid young boys can be—particularly when trying to impress older boys. I tried to outdo my teammates and ate so much watermelon that I ended up sick and threw up all evening. To this day, I can't eat or even look at a slice of watermelon without having dry heaves. Going back to Augustus Gloop, even he had to OD on chocolate at some point. I think I'm close to tapping out on all this 'fun.'"

"I think Alyssa is on her tenth watermelon. As to you—you really are a pussy, Bro." Craig laughed. "Put on your big boy pants and let's drive on. What do you want to do next?"

Pausing for a minute to think, Steve said, "Okay. If we have time before the concert tonight, I'd like to see the 'Volcano.' Can we walk there from here?"

"After our experience walking to the Cal, I don't want to walk anywhere outside in Las Vegas. It's too hot, and the entire town smells like pot. And if we try and get off the main drags to avoid the crowds and take a short cut, we might run into the 'mole people,'" Craig said.

"'Mole people.' What in the hell are you talking about?" Steve asked wide-eyed and confused.

"Those are the homeless people and drug addicts who live in the labyrinth of flood control tunnels burrowed under Las Vegas."

"Are you serious?"

"Yes. One place I read about avoiding is the open-air drug emporium in the wasteland between Caesar's and the Rio Hotel where addicts, drug dealers, and the homeless— many of whom are mentally ill—congregate. Why there? Openings to five of the tunnels are located nearby. Thousands of people live underground. Most linger there during the day to avoid the heat. They have become so accustomed to the dark they apparently have to shield their eyes from the neon lights at the Rio as they emerge at night. Passersby are accosted for socks, meth, or worse. Violence is endemic."

"Did you say 'socks?' I don't get it," Steve said.

"It only rains a handful of days a year in Las Vegas, but when it does, the monsoons can cause flash flooding. The 'mole people' have to evacuate from the tunnels like rats abandoning a sinking ship. Sometimes, they don't get the word of impending rains on the grapevine and actually drown. Socks and shoes are at a premium because the bottoms of the tunnels can remain damp, causing fungus and other nasty afflictions to their feet."

"My God, Craig. It's hard to imagine people emerging from a hidden, subterranean world begging for socks with all the glitter above where the 'beautiful people' sip champagne from a quarter of million dollar Midas bottle.

All I can think of is Martin Luther's comment about mankind being a 'dung-pile covered in snow.'"

"That's a great metaphor, Bro," Craig said. "I return again to Duke's question about what's more twisted: fantasy or reality?"

"A couple of days ago, you mentioned that the people at the Craps tables in the morning are the most interesting because most of them have been there all night; you wonder why, and then try and tease out their individual stories. Can you imagine how many individual stories there must be among the 'mole people?' Why is a person homeless? Why is someone on drugs? Do they have families? If someone is struggling with mental health issues, what, if anything, can be done to help?"

"Interesting and compassionate perspective, Bro. I'm surprised you don't default to the notion of individual responsibility and turn away."

"That's not fair, Craig. Even though I agree with the need for individual responsibility, I would challenge you about who we're talking about. Everyone needs a helping hand at some point, whether it's a lonely elderly person or someone who's sick on drugs or mindless entertainment. Didn't you say the same thing about the help you received to launch your private equity firm? I'm not discounting the individual responsibility of those in the throes of despair, but don't you and I have an individual responsibility to help."

"If only it were that simple." Craig sighed. "I salute your sentiment, but despair at where we're headed as a society and whether anything can help."

The two of them summoned a car from the Bellagio and headed over to the Mirage. The iconic 'Volcano' actually includes two volcano systems, a lagoon, and more than one hundred fire 'shooters' that shoot fire balls twelve feet in the air choreographed to music. It also features waterfalls and surrounding pools with fire and smoke effects. The combination of shooting fire and dancing water, accompanied by music, is dramatic and disturbing.

"This is insane!" Craig declared. "Notwithstanding the name of the resort, this is no 'mirage.' You can actually feel the heat of the fire. One of the real disconnects for me, just like the Bellagio Fountains and many other attractions, is the use of all this water here in the desert. The water in the aquifers is being withdrawn faster than it can be replenished, and so it's like mining—once the water is mined, it's essentially gone. The excess and the parallels with Las Vegas as an idea are disturbing."

Reeling and feeling deeply unsettled, Steve said, "It's definitely not a mirage. I wonder if this is what Hell looks like."

Chapter 8
A Break in the Circuitry

Steve had become increasingly uneasy about all the "fun" they were having in Las Vegas. He had bought into Craig's enthusiasm for 'buying the ticket and taking the ride'—at least for the trip, but the experience was beginning to feel not only like eating too many watermelons, but like the vertigo he had experienced as a kid on certain rides at the county fair where his eyes saw one thing, his muscles felt another, his inner ear sensed something entirely different, and his brain couldn't synthesize the mixed signals—resulting in disorientation, dizziness, and nausea. Just as he would shut down at the fair, he didn't think he could go on in Las Vegas.

Steve told Craig before the concert that he was cutting the trip short. They had left Columbia on Tuesday and originally planned to stay for a week but Steve would now be decamping on Sunday. He had felt completely played out with sensory overload—falling deeper and deeper into the rabbit hole. It wasn't just the disorientation that drove his decision—he couldn't quite identify the foreboding that had enveloped him—but knew he had to go home before there was no way back. In anticipation of the concert they would be attending, he had been thinking about Pink Floyd's song "Hey You" and the line about coming home being a fantasy because the "Wall" was too high. [xxxvii] Craig tried to cajole him into staying a couple of more nights but Steve was resolute. He was embarrassed to reveal the real reason for wanting to leave early and simply said that his daughter, Jennifer, was being bullied on social media and he needed to get home—something Craig readily understood.

"I'm disappointed, Steve, but I get it," Craig had said. "The good news is that we have this last night together. Let's make it memorable."

The concert that evening was by the 'Australian Pink Floyd' cover band at the Virgin Hotel. Both Craig and Steve had been fascinated by the original Pink Floyd, which had launched the acid-rock era with Syd Barrett's LSD-inspired psychedelic music in the late 1960s—about the same time that San Francisco, the then counterculture capital of America, was hosting both Hunter S. Thompson as he chased the American Dream and Jefferson Airplane as they released "White Rabbit." LSD had been both a blessing and curse for Barrett, unleashing his singular creativity but also adding to his schizophrenia—the combination leading to an implosion.

The concert was over-the-top with superb musicians and a stunning light and laser display, video animations, inflatables, a state-of-the-art high resolution LED screen, and other special effects.

Craig and Steve were swept up in the euphoria of the crowd—that magical phenomenon where one plus one equals three like flood-swollen tributaries dumping into a raging river to form a massive wall of water. At the end of the concert, they felt absolutely spent.

"Man, that's one of the best live shows I've ever seen," Craig said.

"I'll second that," Steve said. "I felt like I was on 'uppers' the whole show, and now I'm on 'downers.'"

"Yeah," Craig said. "I know exactly what you mean."

Craig continued, "I think you know that Pink Floyd's 'Wish You Were Here' was dedicated to Barrett, who came up with the name of the band by creating a fusion of his two favorite American blues musicians: Pink Anderson and Floyd Council." [xxxviii]

"I always wondered about the name," Steve said. "Did you learn that in your guidebooks?" he replied tauntingly.

"No, Craig responded with a chuckle." I wondered as well and simply Googled it."

"The album really hit me in the gut," Craig noted. "It made me think for the first time about the detached feeling many people have as they drift through life, withdrawing physically, mentally, and emotionally. I wondered: that couldn't happen to me, could it? The group's masterpiece, 'The Wall,' rubbed my nose in thoughts like abandonment, isolation, and mental fragility—and the desire to seal oneself off—something I had never thought of before. [xxxix] At the time, I found the themes deeply disturbing and even alien—albeit thought provoking. Looking back, I think the group was prescient."

"Maybe," Steve said. "When I finally sat down and read some of the lyrics, I thought they were depressing and even alarming. I have to admit, I took a break from Pink

Floyd for some time. Thinking about it now, I can see that their music was a cry for help—and a warning."

"Well put. I hadn't thought of it as a warning, but of course that's exactly what it was," Craig replied. "A warning of a future that's increasingly become the present."

***

The two of them had spotted the "Double Down Saloon" on their way to the concert. The bar is located one block south of the Virgin hotel. They decided to give it a try on their last night in town.

The Saloon was another off-the-wall "experience," a real dive bar, very dark, with vivid, chaotic murals covering every inch of the walls. Disturbing videos crashed in on them from every angle. Steve wondered out loud if he had a detached retina, a flashback from his experimentation with acid in college, or if this was simply a melding of the many 'altered reality' immersive experiences they had encountered in Las Vegas.

They settled in at the bar and ordered drinks and bar food. A short time after they arrived, the featured all-girl punk band, "The Negative Nancys," went on a break, giving the two of them a chance to talk as they inhaled their toasted quesadillas and quaffed "bacontinis" (bacon-infused vodka martinis served with a strip of bacon), a decadent drink invented at the Double Down.

Craig and Steve kept to themselves, not wanting to make eye contact with a raucous group of sinister-looking badasses who came in just after the band had gone on break and established a beachhead at the far end of the bar. One of the troublemakers was wearing a dog collar dangling an Iron Cross with what appeared to be a superimposed swastika. He also sported a tattoo that shouted the words, "Extreme Violence." Another had a shaved head with tattoos covering most of his face, head, and neck, with metal studs protruding from his scalp.

"What a freak show," Steve whispered to Craig.

"You think?" Craig replied. "It reminds me of the 'Mos Eisley Cantina,' the intergalactic bar in *Star Wars*. [xl]

"Can you imagine interviewing the tattooed guy with the studs for a job?" Steve asked. "What a first impression."

"Are you kidding?" Craig replied sarcastically. "I can definitely see him in a bespoke suit working in an investment bank where client encounters are at a premium. To each his own—I guess."

Just then, one of the badasses, displaying a gap-toothed smile that evoked the image of blown-out windows in a dystopian urban landscape, let out a loud *woop! woop! woop!* mimicking a howler monkey. The others laughed maniacally in response.

"Look at me!" Steve said disdainfully. "Wouldn't you think the piercings and tattoos would be enough?"

"One would think so," Craig replied. As much as he was totally opposed to open carry and concealed weapons, he had to admit—but only to himself—that he felt reassured that Steve was carrying. It was at moments like these that he could understand "Pink's" desire to be walled off from others.

Leaning forward on his stool, steadying himself with both elbows on the bar as he studied his martini, Craig mused, "Duke and Gonzo came to Las Vegas in 1971 searching for the American Dream. Duke thought he had almost grasped the dream with the 'free love,' psychedelic-infused, counterculture movement in San Francisco in the '60s. He came to realize it was nothing but a hallucination—a brief moment in time that had flared brightly but then burned out like the last ember in a dying fire. But he never gave up, continuing to pursue the dream while clinging to a drug-induced haze during his fling in Las Vegas. I loved the line in the book where he said something about riding the rising tide, which seemed unstoppable at the time but just a few years later being able to see how the tide had ebbed. And yet, his longing for the elusive 'Dream' never ended. The last line of the book was about his reincarnation as a sick but confident Horatio Alger."

"The American Dream means different things to different people," Steve said, "and we're all chasing it. To me, at its core is the notion of freedom. The freedom to try and achieve material success for yourself and your family. The ability to enjoy religious, political, and economic freedom. Hell, it's one of the core principles of the Declaration of Independence: 'life, liberty, and the pursuit of happiness.' America has always represented freedom and opportunity to the rest of the world."

"I agree. However, as we've discussed, part of our problem right now as a country is our inability to balance individual freedom with a sense of responsibility to the community—the greater good. It's not just about 'rights' but about 'obligations.'"

"As we've also discussed, one part of those 'obligations' is the individual responsibility each of us has to look in on and take care of our neighbors—particularly the elderly and infirm. We can't slough that off on government, or charities. Such person-to-person interactions are meaningful not just for the person being helped, but the helper as well."

Taking a long drink of his martini as Craig paused in quiet contemplation, Steve said pleadingly, "This is our last night here, Bro. Can we talk about something other than guns, abortion, pronouns, and the notion of a 'Christian Nation?' It's depressing."

Smiling while swilling his martini and signaling the bartender for another, Craig replied, "I agree—with one final thought. Let's put the culture wars to one side— they're just a symptom. The parallels between what Duke and Gonzo encountered in terms of altered reality, the excesses of Las Vegas in general, and what every-day America is experiencing are the main disease."

"What are you talking about? What disease?" Steve sighed.

"Let me use an analogy. In blood cancers, it isn't the cancer itself that kills, but rather the side effects. Red blood cells carry oxygen to organs. Platelets help form clots, slow or stop bleeding, and help wounds heal. Plasma carries nutrients to the body and transports waste to the kidneys and liver, which remove the waste and cleanse the blood. There are multiple types of white blood cells that are key players in the body's immune system. When one type of blood cell is cancerous, it grows uncontrollably, crowding out other blood cells, thereby reducing and even blocking out their necessary functions. Over time, there can be organ failure, internal bleeding, strokes, infections, or other system crashes which ultimately lead to one's demise."

"How do you know this, Craig? I can't remember— did Olivia have a blood cancer?" Steve asked.

"She did," Craig replied, his voice breaking up. "Several of Olivia's systems shut down, and there was nothing the docs could do. There are a number of targeted therapies now that might have saved her, but…"

"I'm sorry, Craig."

"Thanks, Steve. The point of my analogy is that America has a blood cancer and there are no treatments available yet."

"Against my better judgment, how about elaborating for a slow learner like me?" Steve asked.

"Scientists have determined that social media and gaming drive feedback loops in the brain that release endorphins and dopamine, creating the same highs as slot machines, craps, sex, shooting a gun, indulgent eating, and the 'feel good drugs,' turning us all into addicts."

"Wait a minute," Steve said. "Shooting a gun releases endorphins?"

"Apparently so," Craig said. "Look it up."

"My point," Craig said, "is that we're becoming a nation of 'Lotus-Eaters,' content to live in an altered state isolated from reality. [xli] I've read that people binging on video games enhanced by augmented reality have actually reported hallucinations and flashbacks. Research studies have found that hallucinations created by drugs and the altered reality in the emerging 'metaverse' distort mood, thought, perception of self, and the environment. And we ain't seen nothing yet. Deep fake videos. Chatbots that can mimic a real person, spread misinformation, and possibly sap our need to be creative."

Catching his breath as he took a sip of his martini, Craig offered, "I find it instructive that factual mistakes by Chatbots are called 'hallucinations.' It appears that people in general are 'hallucinating,' not being able to differentiate between what's real and what's virtual— what's true and what's fake. Living within illusions in virtual communities. The common result of our addictions—and I include the two of us with our abuse of alcohol on this trip—appears to be altered reality, delusions, and hollow dreams—the very essence of Las Vegas. That's not to say that the culture war 'symptoms' aren't important. They are—and can destroy us—just like system failures in blood cancer victims. But it's the cancer itself that is the core of the problem, and stopping it—or at least controlling its deleterious effects—should be the goal."

"That's a sobering thought." Steve sighed. "Are you sure you're not high on drugs?"

"I may be high on alcohol—but not on street drugs," Craig said, letting out a deep sigh. "At least not yet."

"I thought we agreed that drugs were off the table, Dude. Our parents tried to scare us about marijuana being a 'gateway drug' and we learned that was totally bogus. But the drugs we tried in college are now being laced with really bad stuff. We can't take a chance," Steve replied with a pained expression. "Hell, as you know, large animal tranquilizers are being mixed with street drugs and can cause lesions that lead to amputations. I'd hate to have to call you 'Dickless.'"

Laughing, Craig said, "And I'd hate to be called that. But if we could be sure that the supply was pure, would you be willing to try some drugs at least once on this trip? It's our last night here, and drugs are just another dopamine hit. We might as well sample the entire menu while we're here in Las Vegas—one last card drawing to an inside straight."

"You sound like an alcoholic saying he'll give up drinking after one last bash. How does that advance the goal of stopping or moderating the cancer you describe? As to street drugs, we can't be certain of purity. Would you trust the dealers we met walking to the Cal? Besides, I'm pretty sure I don't want to see giant reptiles ripping people apart with the carpets slimed in blood. And as Duke himself observed, drugs are irrelevant with the altered reality all around us here in Las Vegas," Steve replied.

Finishing his martini and ordering another, Steve said, "As to your thesis that the altered reality in Las Vegas is becoming mainstream, I hear you, but some of it seems like a real stretch. You won't find me wearing a clunky virtual reality headset any time soon."

"The virtual reality industry is in its infancy, Steve. Apple just took a leap forward with its 'Vision Pro' that it describes as 'spatial computing.' Basically, it's a computer that you wear on your face, but the real advance is that the computer is controlled not by a mouse, keyboard, or touch screen but rather by a user interface through eye tracking and gestures. And all kinds of Apps can be added to the platform."

Craig continued, "But put that to one side. A headset isn't necessary. If you haven't done so already, read Neal Stephenson's 1992 sci-fi book *Snow Crash.* [xlii] He coined the phrase 'metaverse,' which reflected his vision about how a reality-based internet might evolve. The book was science fiction but was frighteningly predictive of what's happening all around us today and what's to come, including his description of people he called 'gargoyles' who wore computers, broken up into separate modules hanging on their bodies, allowing them to be plugged into the internet 24/7. My God, Steve Elon Musk has a company called 'Neuralink' that has just gotten FDA approval for clinical trials with humans to implant high bandwidth brain-machine interfaces that connect humans and computers at all times. Among the first intended uses are to allow a person with paralysis to control a mouse, keyboard, or other computer functions like text messaging with their thoughts. It doesn't take a great leap to see where that might lead—with communication working in both directions. Musk himself has talked about putting humans on a path to 'symbiosis with artificial intelligence.'"

"My head is ready to blow up Craig. I'm hoping you're the one who's delusional—not the world around us."

"Las Vegas used to be 'Sin City.' A place where you escaped to indulge your darker impulses. 'What happens in Vegas stays in Vegas.' Not any more. Las Vegas is now celebrated as an 'All-American Town' and is one of the fastest growing metropolitan areas in the country. Just think about the virtual reality of Luxor's 'immersive' experience in King Tut's Tomb. Were you struck by that older woman we met—I think her name was Jean—saying that the Luxor Hotel exhibit was better than the real thing she had recently seen in Egypt?"

"I'll admit that her observation surprised me," Steve replied.

On a roll now like a winning shooter at a Craps table, sounding almost manic even as he slurred his words from too much alcohol, Craig spewed on, "The glitter, gambling, non-stop entertainment, the excess—all mainstream now, satisfying an American public where reality is blurred; boredom has become unbearable; everything is entertainment—no longer a quest for fifteen minutes of fame, but fifteen seconds on Tik Tok where you can star in your own video. Just think about the idiot insurrectionists storming the Capitol and live-streaming incriminating evidence against themselves. Look at the recent incidents at concerts like an audience member throwing a cellphone at singer Bebe Rexha, giving her a black eye and sending her to the hospital for stitches, or at a Pink concert where an audience member tossed her mother's ashes onto the stage—both attention-seekers hoping to go viral. Hell, we experienced it at Knuckleheads. Take a minute and absorb our surroundings here at the Double Down Saloon. This is what America is becoming—with the cancer metastasizing."

"That's a troubling vision, Craig. Thank God those things haven't come to Missouri," Steve said as he drained his martini and ordered another—this time with two bacon strips.

Laughing, Craig said, "Ah, the 'Show-Me' State— where residents rest easy in their belief that when the world ends, they'll have more time because it takes so long for the news to arrive. I know you said you're planning to get more involved, but have you ever checked how much time your kids spend on social media? How many casinos are there now in Missouri? Sports betting, already approved in forty states, is teed up for approval in the legislature. I was shocked to find that recreational pot is now legal in Missouri. If I recall correctly, it was passed by ballot initiative rather than by the legislature because that's what the people want."

"You're giving me a migraine, Bro," Steve said.

"More and more, politicians across the country are becoming performance artists rather than serious people concerned with policy and governing," Craig said. "Misinformation is spread in Missouri just like other states. Most Americans get their news from the internet, podcasts, or certain cable news outlets where truth is disregarded for ratings. Newspapers and responsible journalism are becoming dinosaurs, and most small towns are now news deserts—dryer than Death Valley. People are beginning to believe anything—like Jewish lasers in the sky starting forest fires—which means they believe in nothing at all, thereby paving the way for the authoritarian strong man, the Anti-Christ on the white horse. [xliii] Ask Tammy about that. Sorry, Steve, it may not be full-blown yet but it's coming to Missouri."

"I hate to share this with you in your state of mind, but what the hell?" Steve said. "Last semester, I asked my students—all under thirty—where they get their news. To the extent they get any news at all, most rely on social media. One student mentioned an amateur anchor on Tik Tok posing as a cartoon fish. Another Tik Tok anchor gives a roundup of the 'fucking news.' As long as it's fast and short, they'll listen—news by sound bite. Forget about background or analysis."

"News from a fish," Craig replied with a sigh. "God help us."

After staring at the temporarily quiet 'Atomic Video Jukebox' for a few moments deep in thought while the two of them remained silent, Craig asked, "Is the American Dream ever achieved? Or are we like Wile E. Coyote endlessly pursuing the Roadrunner and realizing, once his elusive prey is finally caught, that his purpose in life is over?" [xliv]

Raising his voice, Steve said, "Are you shitting me? Give me a break, Craig. Hell, you've achieved the American Dream—great material success and, with that, total freedom to do whatever you want that makes you happy."

"I made fifty million dollars by the time I was twenty-nine," Craig replied. "At that point, in an industry where success is measured by how many dollars you accumulate, what's the goal? One hundred million? A billion? What's the point?"

"Oh my God. Let me take out my violin. I'd love to stand in your shoes, dude. Reinvent yourself for Christ's sake. You're a smart guy. Create a company that makes a difference. Get involved with philanthropy. Run for Governor. Unlike me—for you the possibilities are endless."

"Maybe," Craig said as he finished his martini—catching himself as he almost slid off his bar stool.

"Boy, that was graceful." He laughed.

"Are you okay, Craig?" Steve asked, concerned that Craig had consumed one too many. Chuckling, he continued, "I just had a disturbing vision of you being fitted for a drool cup in your dotage."

"Thanks, Pal, but I'm fine," Craig said. Laughing, he added, "As to one day being in my dotage, like Thompson, I don't think I have any interest in living past fifty."

Glancing at the bar menu, Craig asked, "How about trying something featured here called 'sweet and sour shots'? Or a hit of acid before we head back tomorrow?"

"No acid for me," Steve replied. "I'll try some shots, but I'm going to call it a night once the band finishes its next set. It's late, and I'm tired. I think you should join me."

"I have one last dance in me," Craig said. "Thanks for coming on this trip, Bro. It's been very meaningful to me."

"For me too, Bro. For me too," Steve said as he toasted Craig with a shot as he realized that he was no longer Sancho Panza the faithful sidekick, but Sancho Panza the realist, and that for his friend, the American Dream was—like the horizon they had marveled at driving west—just beyond his reach.

***

Steve got back to the room around midnight. He was bleary-eyed and couldn't remember if Las Vegas was one or two hours behind Missouri. Either way, he was pretty certain that Tammy would be asleep but called anyway, dialing the land-line rather than her cellphone that would probably be turned off. What he had to say had been bubbling up inside him like a kettle on the boil, and he just couldn't wait. The phone rang half a dozen times before she picked up.

"Hi Tammy. Sorry to call so late. What time is it there? Did I wake you?"

"That's okay. It's two in the morning here. Is everything all right?"

"I think so, Tammy. I've been doing a lot of thinking."

Steve grew quiet, searching for the right words.

After a silence that lasted for seconds but seemed like minutes, Tammy asked, "Are you still there, Steve?"

"Yes, I'm still here." Hesitating, he finally blurted out, "I believe you know that I've been very unhappy. My career sucks. I hate to say it, but you and I seem to have lost the spark long ago. The kids don't respect me, and I don't respect myself. I want to make a change."

Pausing for a moment while she gathered herself, her focus now laser-sharp, Tammy said, "What are you saying, Steve? Do you want a divorce? If so, this is a pretty shitty way to let me know. I should have known that you spending time in Las Vegas with the Pied Piper wasn't a good thing."

"No, no, no, Tammy. Just the opposite!" Steve protested. "This trip has been a revelation for me. I've come to realize that I'm the problem. Do you hear me? **I'm the problem**! Will you give me a second chance?"

Without hesitation, Tammy said, "Of course I will, Steve. I would love a second chance as well."

"Is it too late with the kids?" he asked plaintively.

"It's never too late, Steve. I know you laugh at my poetry group but there's a wonderful poem by Seamus Heaney that comes to mind. It's called *When all the others were away at Mass* and illustrates beautifully that what kids want and treasure, and remember most at the end, is time alone with a parent. I'll share the poem with you when you get home, but Heaney's insight, as he sits at his mother's deathbed, is captured by his memory of the simple act of peeling potatoes alone with his mother while all the others were in church. He paints an evocative picture of the two of them, with her head bent toward his, their breaths commingled, all hers in that moment." [xlv]

"I desperately want to connect with the kids, Tammy—and reconnect with you—and be thankful for all of our blessings and what we are, not what we'll never be."

"Me too, Steve. Come home safely. We have a lot of catching up to do. Godspeed."

With that, Steve crawled into bed and passed out. He slept more deeply and soundly than he had in years knowing that tomorrow was a new day.

Chapter 9
The American Dream

The pounding in his head was relentless. Thud! Thud! Thud! As he drifted in the ether between sleep and near-sleep, Steve was clear about one thing: no more 'bacontinis' or 'sweet and sour shots' for him. No more excess of any kind. *My flight isn't until mid-afternoon,* he thought. *I need to get some more rest so I have a clear head when I see Tammy.*

But the pounding persisted. As some point, the fog lifted slowly in his prefrontal cortex, and he realized that the sound wasn't coming from inside his head but from the door to his room.

"Just a minute," Steve bellowed. Dragging himself out of bed and pulling on a shirt and pants from the pile on the floor where he had stripped the night before, he stumbled to the door and opened it.

"Mr. Ehrlich? I'm Detective Del Toro from the Las Vegas Metropolitan Police Department. I believe you know Mr. Maguire from the Bellagio. May we come in?"

Disoriented, Steve forced out the words, "Of course."

As he struggled to get his bearings, Steve's impression was that the door behind Del Toro and Maguire was pulsating in and out like a dying being gasping for air. It occurred to him that the imagery he was seeing represented the raccoon he had so perseverated on becoming roadkill. *Is this really happening or just another illusion? Am I in the middle of a nightmare?"*

Focusing on the two men in front of him, Steve finally asked, "What's up?"

"When did you last see Mr. Wells?" Del Toro asked.

Confused at first, Steve looked around the room and realized that the other bed hadn't been slept in.

"We were at the Double Down Saloon last night after a concert at the Virgin Hotel. Since I decided to head home today, I called it an early night. I got here around midnight. Craig decided to stay out. Why are you asking? Is everything okay?"

"Are you sure it was midnight when you got in?" Detective Del Toro asked.

"Yeah. I checked the time before calling my wife in Missouri because I knew it would be late there. She pointed out that it was two in the morning Central Time."

"Why did you call so late?"

"I wanted to talk with her about coming home today rather than Tuesday as originally planned. Why do you ask? What's this about? Is Craig okay?" Steve asked as alarm bells quickly drowned out the pounding in his head.

"Did you make the decision to come home after you left Mr. Wells, or earlier?"

"Earlier. I told Craig about it before the concert."

"What did you do after the concert?" Del Toro asked.

"As I mentioned, we went to the Double Down Saloon right near the hotel."

"Why did you decide to cut the trip short?" Del Toro asked.

"I'd had enough. I was on overload and just couldn't take any more 'fun.'"

"Mr. Ehrlich, did you leave your room after calling your wife?" Del Toro asked.

"No. I was tired, and—to be honest—a little drunk. I crashed."

Getting agitated, Steve demanded, "I'll ask for the umpteenth time—what's this about?"

"I'm sorry to tell you this, Mr. Ehrlich, but Mr. Wells was found floating face down in the Bellagio Fountains at daybreak this morning. It appears that he died sometime overnight."

The pronouncement hit Steve like a sucker punch, knocking him out of his stupor and delivering a numbing clarity. "Are you shitting me?" he protested, absolutely stunned by the news. "Are you sure it's him?"

"I'm afraid so. Mr. Maguire was able to identify Mr. Wells. He had made a point of getting to know Mr. Wells because the resort held him is such high regard."

"I'm so sorry for this horrible news, Steve. I'm sick to my stomach," Maguire said looking absolutely morose, the blood having drained from his face.

Steve tried to steady himself but tripped on one of the shoes he had left on the floor and fell backwards onto the bed. Slowly righting himself and sitting on the side of the bed, he cried out, "I can't believe it. How did it happen?"

"That's what we're trying to figure out," Del Toro replied. "His wallet was on him with several hundred dollars so we don't think there was a robbery. There were no visible signs of trauma. It's possible that he simply slipped and fell into the Fountains and drowned. We'll do a post-mortem but, at first blush, we're mystified."

Del Toro continued, "We did check the logs of the Bellagio car service since you and Mr. Wells were frequent users. There is a record of you taking a car from the Double Down to the Bellagio at eleven-forty last night. We also reviewed security tapes from the Bellagio that show you coming in shortly thereafter. There's no record of Mr. Wells using the car service or entering the Bellagio."

"Wait a minute," Steve, blurted out, his mind reeling. "Why would you check the car logs and security tapes? And since you knew when I got in, why would you ask me? Am I a suspect?"

"We're simply doing a thorough investigation, Mr. Ehrlich. It would have been negligent for us not to check car logs and security cameras for both you and Mr. Wells and to cross reference that with your recollection. At this point, you're not a suspect; we don't even know if there's been foul play. We'll also be checking with taxis to see if anyone remembers transporting Mr. Wells late last night as well as the bartender and wait staff at the Double Down to see if anyone recalls anything. The post-mortem, which will include toxicology tests, should help us determine the cause of death and next steps, if any."

"Do you know if Mr. Wells had any health problems?" Del Toro asked.

Grappling to regain his equilibrium like a swimmer who had gone too deep and exploded to the surface in a near panic gasping for breath, Steve spit out, "Not to my knowledge."

Pausing, Steve continued, "I haven't seen Craig in twenty-five years. We went to college together at the University of Missouri, and he came up with the idea of this trip. As far as I know, he was completely healthy. He looked great—very physically fit."

"Do you know if he was depressed or had any suicide ideation?"

"I don't think so, but again, I haven't been involved in his daily life. We talked infrequently."

"Do you know if he had money problems?"

"To the contrary. He mentioned at the bar last night that he had made so much money that he wondered out-loud about his purpose in life, but I didn't get the impression that he was depressed. He struck me as being full of life and having a great time."

"Did the two of you get back to the hotel together the other nights you were here?"

"Yes. I was tired last night and was thinking about going home. Craig said something about having one more dance."

"What do you suppose he meant by that?" Del Toro asked.

"I assumed he just wanted to have some more fun in Las Vegas before hitting the sack and heading home today," Steve said.

"Why did the two of you decide to come to Las Vegas in the first place?"

"It was Craig's idea. We both loved Hunter S. Thompson's book and wanted to see what Las Vegas was like fifty years after the book was published."

"Did that include the use of drugs?" Del Toro asked.

"No," Steve answered.

"How about Mr. Wells? Did he use any drugs?"

"He didn't—at least not while I was with him."

"Could he have used last night after you separated?"

"I don't think so but obviously can't say for sure. We had talked about not taking a chance because of fentanyl and other adulterations."

"So you talked about using drugs?" Del Toro asked as he looked closely into Steve's eyes.

"Only in the sense that we had pledged to my wife that we wouldn't follow in Duke and Gonzo's footsteps in that regard."

"But you can't be certain that your friend didn't use drugs last night after you came back to the hotel," Del Toro said.

"I can't be certain. I guess the post-mortem will answer that question."

"You mentioned that you were a bit drunk last night. How about Mr. Wells?" Del Toro asked.

"We both had a lot to drink. I have a pounding headache right now and feel nauseous. I'm not sure if the nausea is because of the drinking, the news of Craig's death, or both."

"Was Mr. Wells drunk when you left him?"

241

"He was clearly buzzed, but he didn't seem any different than other nights we were together. We weren't driving, and I had no problem calling the car service. I assumed that Craig was in a similar state."

"Did Mr. Wells have a family or someone we can contact?"

"He had been divorced twice with no children. I know the second divorce was quite acrimonious, so I suspect there has been no contact there. He had a sister he was very close to, but, tragically, she died of cancer our junior year in college. It was very tough on Craig, but he soldiered on. I know her death fractured an apparently already tenuous relationship between his parents, which led to divorce. They've both passed on at this point."

"Do you know if he had any other relatives or someone he was close with—someone we can contact?"

"I'm sorry to say that I don't. Craig was so gregarious that there must be lots of friends; I just don't know who they are."

Thinking for a minute, Steve said, "I know his private equity firm, which is based in Manhattan, is called 'Tarpon Holdings.' I don't know the number, but I'm sure you can Google it."

Feeling a tremor run through his entire body as he looked up at Del Toro, Steve asked, "Do you need me to verify Craig's identity?"

"No," Del Toro said as he wrote briefly in his notepad. "That won't be necessary. His wallet had his driving license with a picture, and Mr. Maguire was clear it was him."

"Thank God," Steve said, breathing a sigh of relief. "Seeing him on a morgue slab would be very tough for me."

Pausing for a minute and taking a deep breath, Steve asked, "What happens now?"

"We'll do the post-mortem." Checking his notes, Del Toro continued, "We'll get in touch with Tarpon Holdings and figure out who is handling his affairs. I suspect that there's a lawyer involved with his personal matters. I'm truly sorry to have to drop this on you, Mr. Ehrlich. And I'm sorry for your loss. Let me give you my card and get all your contacts."

"Of course," Steve said, still staggered in disbelief.

"We'll be collecting all of his personal items, like clothes, suitcase, or duffel bag, and the like," Del Toro said. "Once we make contact with his representatives, they can decide what to do."

"Craig owned a 1973 Chevrolet Caprice that the valet parked," Steve noted.

"Thanks. We'll take possession of the vehicle as well," Del Toro replied.

"Please accept my sincere condolences, Steve," Maguire said, "and let me know if there's anything I can do for you."

"Thanks, Tobey," Steve replied.

Pausing to consider the enormity of what had happened, Steve muttered, almost inaudibly, "I have a flight home scheduled for this afternoon. Craig was my friend. It doesn't feel right leaving him here alone."

Putting a hand on Steve's shoulder in a reassuring gesture, Detective Del Toro replied, "Understandable—but there really is nothing you can do at this point."

He knew that Del Toro was right, but all Steve could think of was Olivia abandoning Craig. Now he was doing the same.

As an afterthought Del Toro observed, "I couldn't help but notice that Mr. Wells' driver's license indicated that he was only forty-seven years old. That's much too young to have this unfortunate end."

Feeling his own mortality crashing down on him, Steve said, "It is too young. I just don't know what to say other than that I'm devastated. Will someone notify me of the cause of death? I'll also need any contact you turn up so I can attend his funeral."

"Of course," Del Toro said. "Once we have all the facts, we'll be in touch."

"Thank you, gentlemen," Steve said as he cupped his face, overcome with disbelief and a grief that was rapidly cascading down to a bottomless pit.

After the two men left, Steve collapsed back on the bed and sobbed. His head was ready to explode. Every tendon, every muscle, and every bone in his body felt the full weight of his forty-seven years and legacy of failure. And now he had failed again—Craig would be alive if he had stayed up and been with him.

What had happened? Had Craig gotten high on street drugs that were laced with fentanyl? Did a combination of drugs and the vast quantity of alcohol they had consumed create a toxic cocktail? Was he drunk and stumble—he had almost fallen off the bar stool and had been slurring his speech—hit his head and drown in the fountains that he had been so fascinated with?

Is it possible that his stated "lack of purpose" and despair at what is happening in America cause him to actually commit suicide? Trying to remember his actual words, did Craig say he wanted one more dance or a 'last dance?' Steve's mind was suddenly flooded with the disturbing video featuring Kim Basinger in Tom Petty's "Mary Jane's Last Dance." [xlvi] And what about his cryptic references to Midas and Wily E. Coyote?

He thought about Craig's description of the relationship with his parents as 'transactional.' *Isn't that how Craig had approached at least his second marriage? And what about his offhand comment about being his parents' son? Had Craig become his parents incapable of a close relationship—never getting to a dreamlike kiss under the glow of a meteor shower.? Was his material success merely "fool's gold?"*

Oh my God, Steve thought. *Hunter S. Thompson committed suicide—leaving a suicide note with a header that was so him: "Football Season is Over." Thompson pulled the trigger with those closest to him nearby: his wife on the phone; his son, daughter-in-law, and grandson in the next room. Is that what this trip was about? Was I actually one of the people closest to Craig after all these years? Did he really have no one else? Had the "wall" become too high for Craig to climb? If so, why didn't I see it? Did I let my hero worship cloud my judgment?*

Craig had quoted Thompson approvingly about not wanting to live past fifty. Steve remembered that Thompson's quote added something about arriving at death totally spent shouting, "What a ride!"

After lying on the bed for what seemed like forever, Steve rushed to the bathroom and vomited, hanging on the toilet with unremitting dry heaves. He finally pulled himself together, showered, dressed in clean clothes, and brushed his teeth several times trying to get rid of the bad taste that he just couldn't seem to expunge. The enormity of Craig's death and the sickening knowledge that the police had considered him as possibly culpable were a crushing weight. He called Tammy, who had just returned from religious services and a picnic lunch at the church, to tell her the bad news. She was shocked and promised to pray for Craig. "I'm so sorry, Steve. I know how much you looked up to Craig and admired him. Please come home safely."

Steve walked down to the Bellagio Fountains just before noon. Craig had told him that, in Spanish, "Las Vegas" means: "The Meadows." It was named by a Spanish trader in the early 1800s who encountered an area of lush meadows resplendent with wild grasses fed by ample water from artesian springs that percolated up from the aquifer. He stared into the twenty-two million gallon Lagoon in the middle of the desert that was filled from a deep well tapping into the aquifer. The symbolism was fraught: water drained from the quickly depleting aquifer (as well as from an exhausted Lake Mead) will spell the ultimate doom of Las Vegas, but not before burning out like a supernova shouting, like Thompson, and possibly Craig, "What a ride!"

As he stood there, the Fountain show began with a thousand fountains shooting water hundreds of feet in the air. *What a waste*, he thought. *Just like the ending of Craig's life and the unlimited promise of what might have been.*

He looked over at the fake Eiffel Tower. He thought about the lost souls at the early morning Craps tables in the smoke-filled casinos all over Las Vegas and the "mole people"—all their individual stories drowned in a dehumanizing statistic and pejorative descriptor; the canals at the Venetian; the "High Roller" Ferris wheel; the erupting Volcano at the Mirage; the Luxor light; trapeze acrobats flying over the gaming tables at Circus-Circus during Duke and Gonzo's time in Las Vegas fifty plus years ago; the "immersive" experiences at any number of sites and rampant altered reality; the Viva Vision Light Show on Fremont Street and the zip line ride into the heart of the mind-blowing visuals; the excesses everywhere from Fremont Street to The Strip and the giant, ominous eyeball from the Sphere that would loom menacingly over the City. He even thought about the desperate characters in the movie *Leaving Las Vegas* and John O'Brien, the author of the semi-autobiographical book on which the movie was based, committing suicide after he had signed away rights to the book. [xlvii]

My God, he thought. *Was Craig right? Is this what's happening to the American Dream? Is this what America is becoming? Did his despair at not being able to withstand the tsunami cause him to cash in his chips? Did Craig surrender, no longer resisting being swept up by the tsunami, and drown in the tidal wave?*

Arriving at Harry Reid International Airport, Steve paused and looked back at the Vegas skyline. The airport was full of party-goers—arriving and departing—underdressed in floral shirts, shorts, flip flops, T-shirts, sweatpants, and other casual gear—a vivid example of depreciating American cultural norms in a mindless race to the bottom. The new arrivals would soon learn that there's a dress code at most clubs. On his way to his departure Gate, he wandered aimlessly by the slot machines 'showing a little leg' to seduce passersby. His flight, which was supposed to leave at 3:30 p.m. was delayed. *Geez*, he thought, *although a small thing in the big picture, can anything else go wrong today?*

Four agonizing hours later, the flight boarded. Steve called Tammy, as he had when first encountering the delay. It was a three hour flight but because of the difference in time zones, he would now be getting in very late. He had so much to talk with her about and wanted to be fresh. Seated in a window seat, at liftoff he glanced down one last time at the valley and saw the Luxor light reaching to the heavens—forever searching—for what? He wondered if the "mole people" were beginning to emerge from their subcutaneous world that was hidden like a diseased circulatory system just below the botoxed, bejeweled face of Las Vegas.

Steve couldn't erase the image he had of Craig floating face down in the Fountains or their conversation about oases in Death Valley—happiness surrounded by sadness—a metaphor for Las Vegas itself.

He reached into the backpack he had placed under the seat in front of him to retrieve the copy of *The Great Gatsby* he had packed. Steve clutched the book for a moment and then turned to the highlighted last page. He realized it was an epitaph for Craig:

"Gatsby believed in the green light, the orgiastic future that year by year recedes before us. It eluded us then, but that's no matter—tomorrow we will run faster, stretch out our arms farther... And one fine morning—so we beat on, boats against the current, borne back ceaselessly into the past." xlviii

Steve reflected on his earlier ruminations about which one of them had taken the right path. Craig had bought the ticket and taken the ride—a man who had everything but, seemingly, nothing at all.

As the airplane gradually ascended on its climb to thirty-five thousand feet, Steve thought about his friend and the profound impact this trip had on each of them. As he looked at the horizon and the now setting sun, he caught a flash of light in the corner of his eye. He didn't know if it was the aura of a nascent migraine headache that haunted him from time to time or the 'green flash,' one of the illusions Craig had been chasing. Steve closed his eyes to the flash and thought about home.

ENDNOTES

[i] *Fear and Loathing in Las Vegas* is a book by Hunter S. Thompson published by Random House in 1972. The book first appeared with the author listed as 'Raoul Duke' in *Rolling Stone* magazine, issue 95, November 11, 1971, and issue 96, November 25, 1971.

[ii] "Permanent Reminder of a Temporary Feeling" is a song written by Jimmy Buffett released in 1999 as part of the album "Beach House on the Moon."

[iii] *American Graffiti* is a 1973 coming-of-age film set in Modesto, California in 1962 featuring the "cruising" and early "rock 'n' roll" culture experienced by the film's director, George Lucas. The film was written by George Lucas, Gloria Katz, and Willard Huyck, produced by Francis Ford Coppola, and starred Richard Dreyfuss, Ron Howard, and other notable actors.

[iv] "No sympathy for the devil; keep that in mind. Buy the ticket, take the ride... And if it occasionally gets a little heavier than what you had in mind, well... Maybe chalk it up to forced *consciousness expansion*: Tune in, freak out, get beaten." *Fear and Loathing in Las Vegas.*

[v] The "7 Mountain Mandate" is a "dominionist" conservative Christian movement that seeks dominion over the seven spheres of society: family, religion, education, media, entertainment, business, and government—with no separation between Church and

State. Its followers believe there are biblical mandates to their goals. Verse 9 from Revelation 17:1–18 states: "And here is the mind which hath wisdom. The seven heads are seven mountains." They believe that their mission of taking over the world is sanctioned by Isaiah 2.2: "Now it shall come to pass in the latter days that the mountain of the Lord's house shall be established on the top of the mountains." The 2013 book *Invading Babylon: The 7 Mountain Mandate*, written by Lance Wallnau and Bill Johnson, added impetus to "dominionism," which has been circulating since the mid-1970s. It was originally regarded as a "fringe" movement but is now becoming mainstream on the Christian right. The "New Apostolic Reformation" movement espouses similar goals.

vi "Kansas City" is a rhythm and blues song written by Jerry Lieber and Mike Stoller in 1952. First recorded by Little Willie Littlefield in 1952, it became a hit when recorded by Wilbert Harrison in 1959.

vii *How the South Won the Civil War: Oligarchy, Democracy, and the Continuing Fight for the Soul of America* is a book written by Heather Cox Richardson published in 2020 by the Oxford University Press.

viii Genesis 19:34 and Genesis 19:35.

ix "Smooth" is a song performed by Santana and Rob Thomas of Matchbox Twenty, written by Itaal Shur and Rob Thomas. It's the lead single in Santana's 1999 studio album "Supernatural."

x "Stars Fell on Alabama" is a song written in 1934—lyrics by Mitchell Parish and music by Frank Perkins. The inspiration for the song was a book by Carl Carmer of the same name and year describing a spectacular display of the

Leonid meteor shower that was observed in Alabama in November of 1833. Astronomers estimate that more than thirty thousand meteors per hour bombarded the atmosphere. The song first became a hit when recorded by the Guy Lombardo Orchestra. It has been covered many times including a duet by Ella Fitzgerald and Louis Armstrong. Jimmy Buffett released the song in 1981 on the album "Coconut Telegraph."

[xi] "Just The Way You Are" is a song written and performed by William Martin ("Billy") Joel released in 2010.

[xii] "Spike" is a song from the album "Southern Accents" written by Tom Petty and released in 1985.

[xiii] On May 22, 1856, a member of the House of Representatives, Preston Brooks from South Carolina, attacked Senator Charles Sumner, a Massachusetts abolitionist, on the Senate floor with a steel-topped cane and nearly beat him to death rendering him unconscious. Sumner had addressed the Senate on the explosive issue of whether Kansas should be admitted to the Union as a slave state or a free state with a speech entitled "Crime Against Kansas." After the beating, Porter calmly walked out of the Senate with stunned observers frozen into inaction. Porter survived a House censure resolution, resigned nevertheless, and was reelected.

[xiv] In 1820, Congress passed the so-called "Missouri Compromise," which admitted Maine as a free State, Missouri as a slave State, and made all of the territories north and west of Missouri's border free. The Kansas-Nebraska Act of 1854, which created the territories of Kansas and Nebraska, repealed the "Missouri Compromise" by allowing local popular vote to decide whether slavery would be allowed. Because Northern

abolitionists logically assumed that Kansas would be settled by people from nextdoor Missouri, which permitted slavery, the "New England Emigrant Company" was formed. The Company, headed by Eli Thayer, a Congressman from Massachusetts, encouraged residents of New England to settle in what became the town of Lawrence to build up a local population opposed to slavery. It is probably the only town in America created purely for political reasons. The site selected was called Hogback Ridge, but was renamed Mount Oread after the Oread Institute in Worcester, Massachusetts, a women's college established by Eli Thayer. Pro-slavery men from Missouri crossed State lines to vote illegally in Kansas leading to armed hostilities opening an era called "Bleeding Kansas." Interestingly, the leader of Quantrill's Raiders, who fought on the side of the South, was William Quantrill, originally an Ohio man who was, ironically, a school teacher in Lawrence before the outbreak of the Civil War.

[xv] *Dances with Wolves* is a movie directed by and starring Kevin Costner. The screenplay was written by Michael Blake; the music composed by John Barry and Peter Buffett. It was released by Orion Pictures in 1990. The movie won the Academy Award for Best Picture.

[xvi] "Big Yellow Taxi" is a song written by and performed by Joni Mitchell in 1970 as part of her album "Ladies of the Canyon."

[xvii] "Welcome Back, Kotter" was a sitcom recorded in front of a live studio audience. Gabe Kaplan starred as a high-school teacher in charge of a diverse remedial education class. It aired on ABC from September of 1975 until May of 1979. The show was created by Gabe Kaplan and Alan Sacks. The theme song, "Welcome Back" was

written by John Sebastian, the former lead for the Lovin' Spoonful, and became a Number One hit in 1976.

xviii *Somebody Somewhere* is a comedy/drama TV series written by Hannah Bos and Paul Thureen released by HBO in 2022.

xix *2001: A Space Odyssey* was a 1968 science fiction film directed by Stanley Kubrick adapted from a story from Arthur C. Clarke, with the screenplay written by Stanley Kubrick and Arthur C. Clarke. 'Hal' was the sentient supercomputer that turns against the human crew.

xx In November of 1900, a white girl was murdered in Limon, Colorado. Fifteen year old Preston Porter, his father and brother, who were African American, quickly left Limon. Suspicion focused on them and they were apprehended in Denver. Preston allegedly confessed under considerable duress including threats of lynching all three. The Governor ordered that the three not be brought back to Limon for eight days to let passions subside, but the Sheriff returned them prematurely. The train stopped just outside Limon and a group of up to three hundred whites chained Preston to a vertical steel rail and burned him alive. The father and brother fled to Kansas. The lynching made national news with *The New York Times* and other newspapers condemning this injustice—apparently shocked that such a lynching could take place in the North. A historical marker in Denver erected in 2020 remembers Preston Porter.

xxi "Back in the U.S.S.R." is a song written and performed by the Beatles in 1968 as part of the "White Album."

xxii Matthew 19:12.

xxiii The disparaging term: the "Great Unwashed," was first coined by the Victorian novelist and playwright Edward Bulwer-Lytton in his 1930 novel *Paul Clifford*.

xxiv Quote by Aldous Huxley who was born in 1894 and is the author of *Brave New World*.

xxv Genesis 1:26.

xxvi *Cities of the Plains* by Cormac McCarthy, published by Penguin Random Housein in 1998 as the final volume of McCarthy's "Border Trilogy." The title is a reference to Sodom and Gomorrah.

xxvii "Happiness Is A Warm Gun" was written by John Lennon released by the Beatles on "The White Album" in 1968.

xxviii "If You Could Read My Mind" is a highly personal song written and performed by Gordon Lightfoot about the breakup of his first marriage, written in 1969 and released in 1970 by Warner Brothers in the album "Sit Down Young Stranger." The liner notes of his boxed set, Songbook, confirm that it is "A song about the failure of marriage." It is one of the most covered songs in popular music history performed by hundreds of performers like Barbra Streisand, Olivia Newton-John, Johnny Cash, and others.

xxix "Gimme Shelter" is an anti-war song by the Rolling Stones written by Mick Jagger and Keith Richards. It was released in 1969 during the height of the Viet Nam War as the opening track on the album "Let it Bleed." The song alludes to rape, murder, fear, and the horrors of war. "Gimme Shelter" features guest vocals by American singer Merry Clayton. Clayton sang so hard, with such passion, that her voice cracked and she suffered a miscarriage shortly after the recording session.

xxx *Positively Fifth Street: Murderers, Cheetahs, and Binion's World Series of Poker* is a memoir by James McManus published by Picador in 2003. On assignment from *Harper's Magazine*, McManus was in Las Vegas to cover the trial of Rick Tabish and Sandy Murphy, who were accused of murdering Ted Binion, the son of the founder of Binion's Horseshoe Casino. The trial coincided with the 2000 World Series of Poker held at Binion's. McManus entered the tournament and placed fifth. The title was inspired by Bob Dylan's song "Positively 4th Street."

xxxi "Positively Fourth Street" is a song written and performed by Bob Dylan released by Columbia Records in 1965. The song is assumed to ridicule previous friends in Greenwich Village who were hostile to Dylan for moving from traditional folk styles to electric guitar and who took offense at what they assumed were personal references in the song.

xxxii *Alice's Adventures in Wonderland* is a children's novel by Lewis Carroll where the protagonist falls down a rabbit hole into a fantasy world. It was published by Macmillan in 1865.

xxxiii *Through the Looking-Glass* is a novel by Lewis Carroll published by Macmillan in 1871. It is a sequel to *Alice's Adventures in Wonderland*. Alice climbs through a mirror and into a fantastical world where, just like a reflection, everything is reversed, including logic.

xxxiv "White Rabbit" is a song written by Grace Slick released by Jefferson Airplane in 1967. In English, chasing a white rabbit means to chase the impossible, a fantasy, a dream.

[xxxv] *Charlie and the Chocolate Factory* is a novel by Roald Dahl published in the U.S. by Alfred A. Knopf in 1964 and in the UK by George Allen & Unwin in 1967.

[xxxvi] "Mother's Little Helper" is a song by the Rolling Stones written by Mick Jagger and Keith Richards released in 1966.

[xxxvii] "Hey You" is a song written by Roger Waters appearing in the rock opera "The Wall" released by Pink Floyd in 1979.

[xxxviii] "Wish You Were Here" was written by Roger Waters and David Gilmour released by Pink Floyd in 1975 as the title track on the album of the same name.

[xxxix] "The Wall" is a rock opera written mostly by Roger Waters. David Gilmour receives credit with Waters on five tracks and wrote three alone. The album was released by Pink Floyd in 1979.

[xl] *Star Wars: Episode IV—A New Hope* is a film in the *Star Wars* series written and directed by George Lucas, with music by John Williams, released in 1977.

[xli] The "lotus tree" is referred to in stories from Greek and Roman mythology. It is mentioned in Homer's *Odyssey* as bearing a fruit that caused a pleasant drowsiness and was said to be the only food of an island people called "Lotophagi" or "lotus-eaters." Consuming the blue lotus flower, which contains narcotic alkaloids, may make a person feel "high" and result in a gentle euphoria. Some have compared it to consuming cannabis. It is not

approved for human consumption in the United States. In the *Odyssey*, those who ate the lotus fruit forgot about returning home and only wanted to stay on the island eating lotus fruit. Alfred Tennyson's poem, *The Lotus-Eaters*, describes a group of mariners who, upon eating the lotus, are put in an altered state and isolated from the outside world.

xlii "Snow Crash" is a science fiction novel written by Neal Stephenson published in 1992 by Bantam Books.

xliii Book of Revelation: Revelation 6.2.

xliv "Wile E. Coyote" and the "Road Runner" are two cartoon characters from the Looney Tunes and Merrie Melodies series first appearing in 1949 in the theatrical cartoon *Fast and Furry-ous*. Created by Chuck Jones and Michael Maltese.

xlv *When all the others were away at Mass* is the third sonnet of the eight sonnet *Clearances* written by Seamus Heaney published by Faber and Faber in 1987 as part of the collection entitled *The Haw Lantern*.

xlvi "Mary Jane's Last Dance" is a song written by Tom Petty released by Tom Petty and the Heartbreakers in 1993.

xlvii *Leaving Las Vegas* is a movie adapted from the semi-autobiographical novel of the same name by John O'Brien starring Nicolas Cage and Elisabeth Shue released in 1995. The screenplay was written by Mike Figgis. Cage won an Oscar for Best Actor in a Leading Role. The movie was distributed by MGM/UA Distribution Co. John O'Brien died from suicide after signing away film rights to his novel.

[xlviii] *The Great Gatsby* is a 1925 novel by F. Scott Fitzgerald published by Charles Scribner's Sons.